Murder Not Quite Buried

Also By Murray Moffatt

A Different Kind of Life (Autobiography)

Play

**Murder Best Unsolved*

**Murder Maybe Relative*

**Murder Maybe By Evil*

Murder And No Play

**Murder Sometimes Cold*

**Murder Not Quite Buried*

**A Shane Daniels Mystery*

Murder Not Quite Buried

A Shane Daniels Mystery

A Novel by

Murray Moffatt

ISBN: 978-1-7782065-5-9

Cover Image: Laura Power, Hailey Power

Author's Note:

'Murder Not Quite Buried' is my fifth novel featuring Shane Daniels, Emma Carstairs and the always colourful and controversial Ben Chen.

In each of those previous novels, I have tried to explore a different theme, including the nature of evil, revenge, greed and even family.

When I first conceived and developed the outline for this latest novel I really didn't have a theme, just three storylines I was anxious to get down on paper. However, when I was about half way through writing the first draft, I realized that 'Murder Not Quite Buried" was a story about relationships, both good and bad. That was the theme. Relationships that end with murder and relationships that change people and result in something they didn't expect.

I hope you enjoy following Shane, Emma and Ben as new and old relationships affect their lives.

Once again, I want to extend a sincere thank you to everyone who has taken the time to read my novels and for all of the support and encouragement of my retirement hobby.

As always, my love and appreciation for my wife Jill who does the thankless job of proofreading my work and to my daughters, Sarah and Laura, for their love and support.

This is a work of fiction. Names, characters, places and incidents are all products of my imagination. Any resemblance to actual events, locations, organizations or persons, living or dead, is entirely coincidental. Any mistakes are mine alone.

For my brothers and sisters: Alayne, Larry, Raymond, Judy, Donna, Catherine, Shawn and Kelly. All unique and talented individuals.

"Happiness often sneaks through a door you didn't know you left open."

John Barrymore

"You can't go back and change the beginning,
but you can start where you are and change the ending."
C.S. Lewis

"It isn't what we say or think that defines us, but what we do."

Jane Austin

Chapter One

Frank Dixon knew that what he had found on that beautiful August evening would haunt him for the rest of his life.

It was an image he already couldn't erase from his mind. He compared it to an earworm that everyone suffers from time to time; a song you hear that starts playing over and over in your head, even if you never liked the song to begin with.

But in Frank's case, this was much worse than an earworm, which eventually fades away. The image of what he saw in the woods continued to linger in the back of his mind and on too many occasions over the past twelve hours, it was dominating his thoughts.

Frank was an eighty two year old retired dairy farmer who sold off his herd of Holsteins and his milk quota over twenty years ago when he got tired of the early mornings and long days for little financial return, primarily because his operation was too small. If he was going to stay in the milk business, he needed to substantially increase the size of his herd, modernize his equipment and obtain a larger quota. But Frank decided he didn't have the wherewithal to make that happen, so he sold everything and called it quits.

But Frank didn't want to leave the place he had called home his entire life. The one hundred acre farm, located ten kilometers outside the southwestern Ontario village of Paisley, had been in the Dixon family for three generations and although his two sons, both with families of their own and living elsewhere in Ontario, never had any interest in becoming farmers, Frank wanted to keep some of the property in the Dixon name.

Mennonite families had bought most of the farms adjacent to Frank's and they were operating large-scale cattle, pig and cash crop operations. They jumped at the chance to add the Dixon property and agreed to let Frank retain a quarter acre section, which included the house and a driveway access.

Frank hoped to finish out the time he had left on earth living in the only home he had ever known. His wife, Mary, had passed away five years ago, so it was just him and Rex, his ten year old dog. Rex was a mutt, but primarily a German Shepard and Lab mix and ever since Mary died, he was never very far from Frank's side. There had been one recent exception. For the past month, every time Frank let Rex out in the morning to relieve himself, the dog would disappear for about an hour. Frank noted Rex always seemed to be making his way to the wooded area at the back of the property next door.

Out of curiosity, when he and Rex went out for their usual after dinner walk last evening, Frank decided that instead of their normal route, he would take the dog to the wooded area to see what had been grabbing the animal's attention.

Rex was a digger, much to his late wife's chagrin, because he was constantly digging in her beloved flower beds, either to bury something or dig for something he thought he could smell in the ground. And it was, unfortunately, not always about bones. Once, one of the cats that lived in the barn died and Frank buried it in the soft ground at the side of the building. But he obviously didn't bury it deep enough because a few hours later Rex dug up the body and left it on the front steps of the house.

Frank enjoyed walking, but his pace had slowed considerably in recent years and the distances he could cover were getting shorter because arthritis was now a problem in both his hips and knees. If he went too fast and too far, he suffered for it when he tried to get to sleep at night and he was stubborn enough not to become reliant on daily doses of pain reliever.

The walk across his property and into the adjacent wooded area would be the farthest Frank had ventured in several weeks, but he was curious to see what had captured Rex's attention recently. The dog was excited about the journey because Rex, who was no spring chicken either, had run ahead of Frank into the woods instead of staying his usual position at the elderly man's side.

Frank was aware of the wooded area's infamous history. It was well known around Paisley that the bodies of two women had been found buried just inside the edge of the forest. They were discovered decades apart by the same man, Shane Daniels, who grew up in Paisley and was now quite a celebrity in the area because he solved the murders of both women, one of them being his mother. And not long ago, Daniels had solved the murder of an elderly Paisley woman who another village resident had been accused of committing.

Frank walked into the woods along a narrow but well-established trail and immediately began swatting at the mosquitoes that had quickly formed a cloud around his head. As he walked along deeper into the trees, he couldn't see Rex so he whistled; one short, loud note that Rex was trained to respond to. When the dog didn't appear, Frank whistled again and this time Rex barked once in response. The dog was somewhere deep among the trees to Frank's right, so he left the trail and started making his way toward where the sound came from, but he had to work his way around trees and through thick underbrush.

Frank finally found Rex in a small clearing, the ground thick with brown, shriveled leaves that had fallen from the nearby trees last fall. As he approached the dog, who was digging furiously, its hind section pointed up, head down, paws working in sync, Frank could see that Rex's efforts today and during previous trips to the site had exposed something. When he got close and saw what it was, Frank cried out loud, "Jesus Christ! Rex, get the hell away from there!"

Rex didn't obey and kept digging so Frank stepped forward and yelled again, "Rex, you stupid dog, I said get out of there!"

This time, Rex did what he was told, moving off a few feet from his discovery where he then sat and looked at Frank.

Frank's stomach rolled and hot bile travelled up his throat. The dog had exposed a body that had not been buried very deep and was in a state of decomposition. It was a woman, judging from the long hair and the top of a sun dress that was visible. The unforgettable smell from the putrefaction hit Frank and he quickly turned, bent over, and threw up the contents of his stomach.

As a farmer, Frank had been around death many times because on a farm, the animals die from time to time for many reasons and it's something you learn to deal with. But this was different, this was a human being, and no one could be prepared for what Frank was seeing today.

But the woman's body was not the worst of the horror Frank was looking at. She was on her back and up against her and under her right arm was the body of a young girl, maybe two or three years old, Frank wasn't sure, but it was a girl because her hair was tied with a pink ribbon.

Frank staggered back, unsteady on his feet, bent over again, and heaved, but there was nothing left in his system to throw up. He turned his back to the bodies so he wouldn't have to look at them again and then walked far enough away so that he was no longer in range of the nauseating smell, although Frank thought it had invaded his clothing.

Several thoughts raced through Frank's mind. Who could do this? What kind of sick person kills a woman and a young child, buries their bodies in a forest but doesn't even care enough to dig a deep enough hole?

The rest of last evening and late into the night was a blur for Frank. He had called 911 on his cellphone and then, with Rex now on the leash he carried in his back pocket, he had walked back to the edge of the forest to wait for the police to arrive.

Within two hours after Frank called, there were four uniformed Ontario Provincial Police officers and a plainclothes Detective at the burial site. Because the property leading up to the wooded area was hard and dry, the crop of grain already harvested, the police were able to drive their cruisers right up to the edge of the trees. However, by the time the officers got there and Frank had led them to the burial site, darkness was starting to descend quickly. It was decided that one of the uniformed officers would wait in his cruiser and keep an eye on the area until the morning when a forensics team would arrive to begin working at the site.

OPP Detective, Sgt. Tyson Cornwell, drove Frank and Rex home and the two men sat in the kitchen drinking coffee while Frank explained the circumstances that led to his discovery of the bodies.

Cornwell was a twenty year veteran of the OPP and had been a Detective for the past decade. He kept himself in excellent shape as evidenced by the muscled chest and arms that pushed tightly against his summer weight dress shirt. Cornwell had green eyes and sharp features, kept his sandy brown hair short and parted to the side, and sported a trim moustache.

Cornwell realized that the elderly man sitting across the table from him was still in shock over what he had found in the woods and the policeman was concerned about Frank's health. He offered to take Frank to the Emergency at the hospital in Walkerton, but Dixon refused saying he just needed some rest and time to put what he saw and smelled out of his head.

"Do you have any idea yet who the woman and child are?" Frank asked, his voice shaky with emotion as he thought about the young lives cut short, especially the little girl.

"A quick check showed no recent missing persons reports," Cornwell replied. "But the investigation is just starting."

Cornwell put his thin notebook in the inner pocket of his suit jacket, stood up, and said, "I don't want you to worry about any of that, Mr. Dixon. You've had a shock after seeing something that nobody should have to see and is even difficult for seasoned police officers. As you said, you need some rest. If you wish, I can arrange for someone to come and see you, and help you deal with what you've been through."

"No, that's okay," Frank said, gesturing with his hands. "I'm a tough old bastard. I'll be fine."

After Sgt. Cornwell left, Frank admitted to himself that he really wasn't going to be fine. He needed to shower and to throw out the clothes he was wearing because whether real or not, he could still smell the putrid odour from the bodies. And he could still see the remains of the woman and the child as if it only happened a few minutes ago.

What a nightmare, he thought, and looked down at his dog who was sitting dutifully beside his chair.

"Thanks a lot, Rex," Frank Dixon said.

Chapter Two

Shane Daniels sat patiently on the edge of the padded examination table and looked at the various posters on the walls of the small room.

Many of them were sponsored by drug companies and featured images of various medical conditions while others illustrated yet more diseases you might be suffering from if you had the conditions listed below. Shane figured he was probably like most people waiting in a Doctor's examination room who read the list of symptoms just in case they had some of them.

Shane was tall, well over six feet, with long legs so his feet almost touched the floor as he sat on the table. His height and long reach had helped him become a star basketball player in high school and university, and even though quite a few years had passed since then, he maintained a muscular physique with regular visits to the gym. Shane had dark hair with a bit of gray now showing at the temples, much to his chagrin, blue eyes, and a perpetual five o'clock shadow. His partner, Emma, said he was one of those guys who didn't realize they were very good looking, which she said added to his charm.

As he sat waiting for the doctor to return to the room, Shane contemplated the reason for his appointment. The pain in his damaged left knee was the worst it had been in several years and although he had sworn off painkillers a long time ago, he had reached the point where he was seriously considering going back on them. Shane knew it would be a bad idea because there was a time shortly after his knee was destroyed when he became heavily addicted to both pills and booze, but he was getting desperate. The pain had been a constant companion for a long time but had now reached the point where it was keeping him up at night and affecting his ability to concentrate at work. And even worse, the quick temper Shane had managed to keep mostly under control since he was a teenager was rearing its ugly head on a more than regular basis and he hated the fact that Emma, the most important person in his life, had to put up with the brunt of it.

Shane remembered the night his knee was damaged like it was yesterday because it prematurely ended his job as a police officer, the only career he ever wanted to have.

He was a rookie Constable with the Brantford Police Service and was partnered with his Training Office, Sgt. Charlie Oak, who was now the Chief of Police.

During a routine patrol, they were called to a loud domestic disturbance at a home in Eagle Place in Brantford's south end. When they arrived at the small bungalow, they were let inside by an elderly woman, Vera Armstrong, who was so inebriated she was unsteady on her feet and slurring her words. Oak asked her where her husband, Jack, was and she said they had been drinking and fighting, and he had gotten very angry and had stormed upstairs.

Oak then asked Vera if they had any weapons in the house and she said she didn't know. The veteran officer called up to Jack and asked him to come downstairs so he could talk to him and in response, the elderly man started ranting at his wife, blaming her for calling the cops on him. When Jack finally came downstairs, he was armed with a shotgun and immediately fired at Oak, hitting him in the chest. He then turned to shoot his wife but Shane, who was standing beside the woman, shielded her with his body and pushed her to the floor. When Jack fired the shotgun, the slug hit Shane in the left knee and Shane, who already had his service weapon in his hand, fired at least four shots that hit Armstrong, killing him.

Oak was lucky because the shotgun blast hit his bulletproof vest, probably saving his life. Shane was not so lucky; while the shotgun shell that hit Oak's vest was filled with buckshot, for some reason the next shell was a slug and Shane's left knee was damaged beyond repair, resulting in him leaving the Brantford Police Service on long term disability.

The long recovery, the constant pain, and the loss of his dream career sent Shane into a period of deep depression and a fog of booze and pills. He managed to pull himself out of it thanks to Charlie Oak's intervention and his promise of a job as an Investigator with a prominent local lawyer, Jason Burke, if Shane cleaned himself up.

The only good thing that came out of what happened to Shane was that he met Emma Carstairs at the support group he started attending.

Emma was an amputee who lost her left leg while serving with the Canadian Armed Forces and Shane fell in love with her. Emma is a beautiful woman with a fair complexion, blue eyes, and blonde hair that she always keeps cut very short. The couple live together at Emma's parent's former house in east Brantford and while Shane has made it a tradition to propose every year, they've never married because Emma says she doesn't need a piece of paper to be with someone she loves.

Shane's thoughts about Emma and what happened to his knee were interrupted when the door to the examination room opened and Doctor Bryce Hughes entered. Hughes was Shane's personal physician but also served as an orthopedic surgeon at the Brantford General Hospital. The Doctor was in his late fifties, a rail thin man of medium height and build, pale complexion, green eyes, a hawk-like nose, thin lips and was mostly bald except for a fringe of short, gray hair.

Shane and Hughes exchanged greetings and then the Doctor sat down at a small desk equipped with a computer and accessed Shane's medical file.

"The CT scan shows there's a significant buildup of scar tissue in what's left of your knee and that's why there's been an increase in the dull pain you're feeling," Hughes told Shane. "I know you've had surgery in the past to deal with the scar tissue and you'll require that again."

"I figured it was something like that," Shane responded.

Hughes turned away from the computer screen to face Shane and said, "From what I understand, the only reason you didn't lose your leg from the knee down was because you were turned so the slug hit your kneecap from the side and not straight on. Even so, the damage was significant and aside from a kneecap replacement there was very little left for the surgeon to work with in terms of restoration."

"There was discussion about possible amputation if the healing didn't go well or if I got an infection," Shane said. "They said I should have a total knee replacement, but they weren't sure if there was enough structure left above and below the knee for that to be successful and I could lose the leg anyway, which I was determined not to let happen."

"Shane, I know you've made a valiant effort to rehab the knee and keep up with the exercise necessary to keep it functioning," Hughes said and then added, "You've also managed to live with the pain without resorting to possibly addicting pain medications."

"However," the Doctor continued, "the time has come for you to get a new knee. There have been some significant advancements in recent years in replacement surgery for knees as damaged as yours. I have a colleague who works out of Toronto General Hospital who is probably the best in Canada in doing the surgery you need."

Hughes explained that artificial joints are made of metal and plastic, with the metal parts replacing the damaged thighbone and hip bone, and plastic is used to replace the cartilage on the shin and kneecap parts. He said if the surgery is successful, they would have Shane up and walking in the hospital, he would use a walker for the first couple of weeks, and full recovery would take anywhere between three months and a year.

"Aside from the problems dealing with the significant damage to your leg, one of the other important considerations at the time you were hurt was that you were a young man and knee replacements typically only last between fifteen and twenty years," Hughes said. "You would have needed another replacement well before now and the specialists weren't sure if that was possible even if they were able to do the first one."

Shane didn't speak for a moment as he thought about what the Doctor was telling him. Then he said, "Leaving aside the fact the replacement might not work, I'm concerned about the recovery time. My job depends on me being mobile, so it could be a real problem."

"Yeah, but if it's successful, as I expect it will be, you'll be pain free and hopefully finally free of that," Hughes said, pointing at Shane's cane leaning up against the examining table.

Shane looked down at his cane and then, with a smile on his face, back at Hughes.

"That would be great, of course, but then I'll have to find another way to defend myself," Shane said.

"You've had to use the cane as a weapon?" Hughes asked with a look of curiosity on his face.

"Unfortunately, in the course of doing my job, there have been occasions when I've been forced to do that," Shane said and then added, "Just recently the cane probably saved my life after it stopped a bullet when a murder suspect tried to shoot me."

"Well, Mr. Daniels," Hughes said, "If you get a new knee you'll be able to run away from trouble."

Chapter Three

Emma Carstairs walked down the hallway of the pediatric surgical floor of the Brantford General Hospital, heading for the nurse's station and the woman she was scheduled to meet there.

Emma was wearing blue scrubs because she had just completed her shift as a nurse in the Surgical Department located one floor below. She was exhausted, it had been a very busy day, but she had promised her friend, Psychiatrist Charlene Anderson, that she would meet with a social worker to discuss a young patient.

When Emma reached the nurse's station she saw a young woman standing at the counter with an identification badge on a lanyard around her neck and holding a manila folder in her hand, so Emma assumed it was her contact from Family and Children's Services.

When Emma approached, the woman held out her hand and said, "You must be Emma, I'm Maggie Sawyer from FACS."

As they shook hands, Emma appraised her contact. Maggie was a big woman with a round face and was wearing a lot of makeup, including dark eye shadow, eyelash extensions and bright red lipstick. She had shoulder length brown hair, multiple piercings along the edge of her left ear and both arms were dark with tattoos. But what stood out most to Emma was Maggie's bright green eyes and engaging smile, and Emma had the feeling that this was someone very easy to like.

"Doctor Anderson speaks very highly of you and your work as a volunteer councillor," Maggie said to Emma.

"I appreciate her saying that," Emma responded. "When I first became an amputee I had a really tough time, not so much physically, but mentally coming to grips with it. Doctor Anderson and her support group were a tremendous help to me and I'm just trying to give something back."

"Well, the young girl I was hoping you could help with may be a bit of a challenge," Maggie said.

The social worker then handed Emma the manila folder she was carrying and said, "Here's the file for you to review later. In a room just up the hall is eight year old Lan Pham. Her parents, Duc and Hai Pham, immigrated to Canada from Vietnam two years ago. They were both killed in a car accident two weeks ago on Highway 403 just outside the city toward Woodstock. Lan was in the backseat and was trapped inside the car when police arrived at the scene. Firefighters had to cut her out of the vehicle but it took time. Her right arm was crushed and by the time they got her to the hospital it was too late to save it and it was amputated from the elbow down."

"Did she suffer any other serious injuries?" Emma asked, her heart sinking as she thought about what the little girl had been through.

"Cuts and some serious bruising caused by the seat belt and shoulder harness," Maggie replied and then added, "Honesty, it's a miracle Lan survived because the car was completely demolished."

"So, you would like me to talk to her," Emma stated.

"Well, I was hoping you could try," Maggie said.

Maggie explained that Lan was known to be a very bright, perhaps precocious young girl, but she had been mostly uncommunicative since she arrived at the hospital, which was not unexpected considering the shock she had suffered. After she awoke from the surgery to amputate her arm, Lam asked about her parents and was told they didn't survive the accident. Since then, other than an occasional nodding or shaking of her head, Lan has refused to communicate with hospital staff and has acted very distrustful toward them.

"She's been acting out," Maggie told Emma. "On several occasions, she has pulled the IV out of her left hand with her teeth, knocked over the IV stand, pushed all the buttons on the monitoring equipment so it malfunctions, and dumped her food tray on the floor."

"She's frightened and angry," Emma stated.

"Everyone feels so bad for her and has tolerated her outbursts," Maggie said. "What has made the situation even more tragic is that we've been unsuccessful in locating any of Lan's relatives."

Maggie said a search failed to find any family members living in Canada and inquiries made in the local Vietnamese community have turned up nothing. The Pham's were classified as refugees when they came to the country and the Canadian embassy in Vietnam has been working with the authorities there to try and locate possible family members.

"If we can get her to talk, Lan may be able to tell us about any relatives we can get in contact with," Maggie said.

"I don't know how much luck I'll have, but I can try and connect with her," Emma said.

"I would appreciate that," Maggie responded. "I have some paperwork to do, so I'll be around here when you're done. If you have any luck communicating with Lan, I have some other important information about her situation I can share with you."

"Okay," Emma said and then walked toward the young girl's room. The door to Lan's semi-private room was open and Emma saw that the other bed in the room was empty. The young girl was sitting up, the blankets pulled tightly across her waist, and the first thing Emma thought was how tiny Lan looked even in a narrow hospital bed.

Lan was a pretty girl with light brown skin, an oval face with Asian features, dark eyes and long, straight, black hair. She was staring straight ahead as Emma entered the room and walked up to the side of her bed. Emma noted Lan's right arm, missing from the elbow down, the stub covered in thick surgical gauze and wrapped in a sterile cloth.

"Hi Lan, my name is Emma," she said, but Lan didn't acknowledge Emma's presence and continued to look at the wall at the end of her bed.

"Maggie from Children's Services, who you've met, asked me to drop by and see how you were doing," Emma continued. "If you don't mind looking, I'll show you why Maggie thought we should meet because we have something in common."

Emma took a couple of steps back from the side of the bed so Lan could see her from the waist down and pulled up the left side of her scrub pants to expose her prosthetic leg. Lan didn't look, but Emma waited patiently with her left pant leg pulled up and finally, after a few moments, the young girl turned and looked at Emma's prosthetic.

"I was a lot older than you when this happened, but I know what it's like learning to live without an important part of your body," Emma said. "A terrible thing has happened to you, Lan, and not just with your arm, and I thought maybe I could help."

Lan didn't respond and after briefly looking at Emma's prosthetic she turned her head and started staring straight ahead again. Emma dropped the leg of her scrub pants and assumed her attempt to engage the young girl had failed, but then Lan finally spoke.

"Did other people make fun of you when they saw you didn't have a leg?" Lan asked in a soft voice. "Because that's what's going to happen when I go back to school with no arm."

Only eight years old and already worried about body image, Emma thought, and this poor young girl is probably thinking about that so she doesn't have to think about losing her parents.

"Well, as I said, I was older than you when I lost my leg and I had already finished school," Emma said. "But yes, a lot of my friends started to treat me differently and some boys said hurtful things and didn't want anything to do with me. But I decided I didn't want friends like that anyway and I learned to ignore the boys."

"Besides," Emma added with a smile, "most of those boys were ugly anyway."

Emma thought she saw the start of a smile on Lan's face, but then it was gone and the young girl returned to staring blankly at the end of her bed. She's frightened and not sure how she's supposed to act, Emma thought. Either way, it appeared their conversation was over, so Emma said, "It was nice meeting you, Lan. I'm so sorry about what has happened, but I can tell you're a smart and strong young lady and I know you have a great future ahead of you. And always remember there will be lots of people available to help you, including me."

There was no response from Lan, so Emma turned and started to leave the room, but just as she reached the doorway, she heard a voice behind her.

"You're very pretty," Lan said.

Emma turned back, saw that Lan was looking at her, and replied, "Thank you, Lan. I think you're pretty too."

"Will you come back to see me, Emma?" Lan asked and Emma could see both pain and confusion on the young girl's face.

"You bet I will," Emma said enthusiastically. "I'll be back first thing tomorrow morning."

After Emma left Lan's room she walked back to the nurse's station where Maggie Sawyer was waiting for her.

"How'd it go?" Maggie asked.

"There's no question she's been traumatized and, at first, I didn't think she was going to respond to me," Emma replied. "But she asked me to come back, so I'm hoping we can connect."

"That's great, Emma, thank you!" Maggie said and then asked, "Can I buy you a coffee? There's some more background on Lan's situation that I think you should be aware of."

Emma and Maggie took the elevator down to the ground floor and walked to the Tim Horton's kiosk located inside the hospital. After getting their coffees, they walked down the adjacent hallway to a small empty office that FACS shared with Victim Support Services.

"Lan's situation has been complicated by the circumstances surrounding the accident that killed her parents," Maggie said after the two women had sat down, Maggie behind the desk and Emma on a folding chair facing it.

"Complicated how?" Emma asked.

"The investigating police officer told me there's evidence to suggest the Lan's vehicle was forced off the highway. There was paint from another vehicle found on the crushed driver's door of the SUV."

Maggie told Emma that there were no witnesses who saw the accident, but when all of the traffic stopped immediately after it happened, several people told police they saw two young men, who both appeared to be Asian, looking inside the Lan vehicle. The witnesses said they assumed the two men were trying to help, but instead, they got in a large pickup truck parked on the shoulder of the highway and drove away. An accident reconstruction expert with the Ontario Provincial Police says the wreckage suggests the Lan SUV was side-swiped by a vehicle in the other lane.

"Do you know if the police have any idea about who would do such a thing?" Emma asked.

"Well, this is where it gets complicated and makes me worry about Lan," Maggie answered.

Maggie explained that after Duc and Hai Pham's names were established from the identification they were carrying, officers took a set of keys Mr. Pham had with him and went to the address listed on the ID. They wanted to check to see if perhaps another member of the family lived there and they could be notified about the accident.

The address turned out to be a large, high-end home in a neighbourhood of such houses in north Brantford. There was no answer when the officers repeatedly rang the doorbell and knocked, and after consulting with a superior officer, it was decided they would use Duc Pham's key to gain entry. It was felt it was necessary to go in the house and search for any information that would lead police to family members or even friends of the Phams because, at that point, they only had Lan they could speak to and she was not only recovering from surgery to amputate her arm, but was uncommunicative.

"When the officers went inside the house, they found that it was very sparsely furnished and there were very few personal items, like photographs or even mail," Maggie told Emma. "When they checked the basement, they found a large-scale cannabis extraction lab."

"What, like a grow op?" Emma asked.

Emma was aware that before the sale and use of pot was legalized in Ontario, marijuana was grown illegally in the basements of tens of thousands of houses across the province. The homes were often located in the middle of upscale subdivisions and the operators would drill through the concrete basement wall to secretly tap into the underground hydro line to power the dozens of heat lamps required for the plants. The homes were damaged by the operation; warped floors and walls, and mould. The laws had to be changed so that real estate agents were obligated to inform prospective buyers that a house had previously been used as a grow op.

"No, not a grow op," Maggie answered. "It's a lab where they extract the concentrate from the plants which is then used for vaporizers and edibles. There's a huge demand for it on the black market. More than half the shelf price for concentrate in a legal retail store is taxes so it's cheaper to buy on the street."

"And this lab was in a house where an eight year old girl was living?" Emma said with a mix of astonishment and anger.

"I'm afraid so," Maggie responded and then added, "And this was no small operation. Police seized over six million dollars worth of cannabis resin and lab equipment."

"Unbelievable" Emma reacted and then asked, "So Lan's parents were running the operation?"

"Not likely owning or running it," Maggie answered.

She then explained that Vietnamese gangs were behind a lot of the grow ops when they were flourishing and they've moved on to the extraction labs. The gangs would be using the same strategy; intimidating newcomer families like the Phams into living in the house with the promise of free rent. It's a lot less suspicious if someone is actually living in the home, particularly a young family.

"If I remember correctly, the grow ops were very dangerous to the health of people who were living in them because of the odour and mould. I assume Lan was living in the same kind of danger with the lab in the basement," Emma said.

"Absolutely," Maggie responded. "There's usually an HVAC system of some kind, but the people working in the lab all wear special masks. None are usually supplied to the families living there."

Emma didn't say anything for a moment, just looked down at her coffee and thought about that beautiful young girl in the room several floors above her. What kind of life had she been forced to live? Even if they were intimidated, how could her parents do that to her? Now she faces a life with no parents and a disability.

So what's going to happen to Lan?" Emma asked.

"She's going to be staying here for some time yet," Maggie answered. "Once she's ready, she'll be moved to rehab and since she currently has no family that we know of, I'll apply to have the government cover the cost of a prosthetic for her arm and I'll have to find a foster home for her."

"There's a reason I'm telling you all of this, Emma," Maggie continued. "You're the first person Lan has responded to. Up until now, she's been completely uncommunicative and she has the answers to a lot of questions. We don't know where the Phams came from and how they ended up living in that house. We don't know if Lan has any relatives we can contact. And the police are hoping she'll be able to tell them something about the accident. Were they, in fact, forced off the road and did she see the two men who looked in the car and then left the scene."

"Could Lan be in danger from the people who own that house?" Emma asked.

"We don't know," Maggie answered and then said, "Given what I've told you, it would be completely understandable if you didn't want to get involved."

Emma didn't hesitate with her response. "That traumatized young girl is all on her own and I'm going to help her any way I can," she said.

Chapter Four

Shane Daniels had to do what he called 'the loop' as he searched for a parking spot in front of Burke and Associates on King Street.

Downtown Brantford has two major one-way streets and Shane had turned left on King off one of them, Dalhousie Street, and after not spotting a parking spot had turned left on the other one way, Colborne Street. He went around the block and back onto King and this time found a spot just up the street from the legal firm.

Jason Burke, his boss and owner of the firm, had long promised Shane a parking spot in the small lot at the back of the building, but that had yet to happen.

Shane parked his black Dodge Charger and sat for a moment going through the emails on his phone. The 1969 Charger was his pride and joy; a V8, 383 four-barrel engine capable of producing 330 horsepower, a dark leather interior, racing-style steering wheel and a Hurst gear shift. His father, who recently died in prison, gave Shane the car on his sixteenth birthday and he has kept it in immaculate shape ever since. Doing that had not been cheap over the years with several engine re-builds, replacing the leather upholstery when it wore out, some body work and customized paint job.

While Shane loved driving the Charger, Emma didn't like riding in it, especially in the summer because the air conditioning didn't work and it had poor ventilation. Emma did appreciate the look and design of the classic car, but thought it was a death trap with its lack of safety features, like airbags, and was always trying to convince Shane to rent a storage place for it where he could go and admire it, just not drive it.

After he finished going through the emails on his phone, Shane noted it was pretty quiet in downtown Brantford for a Monday morning. The city, with a population of just over one hundred thousand, was located in southwestern Ontario, a half hour drive east of Hamilton and an hour east of Toronto. It was where Alexander Graham Bell invented the telephone and the hometown of Wayne Gretzky, one of the greatest hockey players of all time. Until the late 1980s, Brantford was known as an industrial town, but the end of that reputation came with the closing of the massive Massey Ferguson combine plant. Some tough economic times followed but today Brantford is often listed as one of the fastest growing communities in Ontario.

Shane set the alarm he had installed in the Charger, the classic muscle car was a natural target for thieves, grabbed his cane, and made his way through the front entrance of Burke and Associates. He stopped briefly at the reception desk to speak to Jill Langley, who had been at the firm right from the first day it opened its doors. In addition to serving as the receptionist, Jill kept the office running smoothly and was considered a bit of a mother figure to many of the young Law Clerks on staff.

Shane went to his office, a rather small room with just enough space for a small desk, two chairs for visitors, and a large, metal filing cabinet.

He didn't mind the small office because he really didn't spend a lot of time in it, preferring to be out working a case.

Shane started up his computer and reviewed his secure, inter-office emails and then checked his office phone for messages. One was from Jason, asking Shane to come and see him when he got in.

Shane walked down to Jason's well-appointed corner office, the door was open, so he knocked lightly on it to get the lawyer's attention. Jason was sitting in the plush leather chair behind his desk, talking on the telephone, but when he saw Shane he waved him in.

Jason Burke was one of the most respected criminal trial lawyers in Ontario and his services were always in demand. He was an imposing figure in the courtroom; a big man, well over six feet tall, with a dark complexion, sharp features and silver hair combed straight back from his forehead. Over the years, his love of gourmet foods had put extra weight on his big frame, but that was not the case in recent weeks. He was still recovering from being shot in the side by a young woman seeking revenge for Jason's involvement in her father's murder trial.

Following surgery to repair the internal damage done by the bullet, Jason convalesced at home for several weeks, doted on by his wife, Gillian. But being a bit of a workaholic, his restlessness was driving Gillian crazy so she finally agreed to let him go back to work.

Shane sat in one of the comfortable chairs facing Jason's desk and when Jason hung up the phone, he asked the lawyer, "How are you feeling? You look good."

"You lie, I look like shit," Jason responded with a smile. "But I don't feel too bad, still a bit weak, and glad to be out of that chair at the house."

"I'm sure Gillie would prefer that you took more time to recover before coming back here," Shane said. Gillie was the name everyone called Jason's wife.

"We made a deal. She let me come back to the office as long as I agreed to only work normal hours," Jason said.

"I'll be interested to see how that works out," Shane said sarcastically. Since starting to work at his firm, Shane and Jason's relationship had developed beyond employer and employee, and they had become good friends. As far as Shane was concerned, Jason had saved him from a life of dependency on pain pills and booze by taking a chance on him and hiring him as an investigator.

"And what about you, Shane?" Jason asked. "How're you holding up since your father's death? It can't be easy dealing with the memories of that part of your life."

"I'm okay, really, that part of my life has been closed and I'm moving on," Shane tried to answer as convincingly as possible.

Shane's mother left him and his father, Ed, when Shane was not quite a teenager and he never heard from her again except for a brief letter she left behind saying she was sorry, but she had decided to leave and start another life. Shane was heartbroken and his father refused to discuss exactly why his mother left them.

When he was seventeen years old, Shane found the body and solved the murder of a young, married Russian immigrant he was having an affair with. Her husband, Max Ivanov, was charged with the murder and it turned out he was actually Shane's Uncle, something his father kept secret from him. Years later, after he had started working for Jason, Max convinced Shane to visit him at Millhaven Penitentiary near Kingston and in a dying declaration said he and Shane's father had made an arrangement; Max had killed Shane's mother and then, in return for doing that for him, Shane's father murdered Max's young wife.

Shane didn't believe Max until he and his friend, Ben Chen, found his mother's body buried in the same wooded area as Max's wife. Ed Daniels was sentenced to life in prison and Shane had refused all contact with him until a prison Chaplain called him and said his father was dying of cancer. His father died in a prison hospice just over a month ago and after a lot of soul searching, Shane decided to bury him next to his mother's grave in a cemetery just outside of his hometown of Paisley. He hoped that with his father's death, a painful chapter of his life was over.

"Just remember, if you ever need some time off, all you have to do is ask," Jason said to Shane.

"It's more than possible I will need to take a leave, but not because of my father," Shane responded. "Depending on what a surgeon in Toronto says, there's a chance I can get a total knee replacement and maybe ditch this thing." Shane held up his cane, which he had leaned against the side of his chair.

"That's great news!" Jason exclaimed. "A leave is no problem, just let me know."

"Thanks, I appreciate that, but until then, I'm good to go," Shane said.

"Well, I have something I'd like you to wrap up for me," Jason said and he pulled a thin manila file from a pile of them on the side of the desk, files Shane figured that had built up during Jason's absence. Although everything in the firm was available on its encrypted server, the legal system still required paper copies of all work products.

After Jason set the file on the desk in front of Shane, he said, "Just over seven years ago, Denise Matheson, a fifty seven year old Brantford woman, disappeared while walking her dog in the Brant Conservation Area where she and her husband, Bernard, better known as Bernie, kept a trailer. It's believed she drowned when she either fell or walked into the Grand River, perhaps to retrieve her dog. Her body was never recovered."

"Because the seven years required under the law has passed, Denise has now been declared legally dead," Jason continued. "The husband, Bernie, can now claim a one million dollar life insurance policy."

"That's an expensive policy. Were the Mathesons wealthy?" Shane asked.

"Not wealthy, but well enough off," Jason answered. "Bernie is an electrician and Denise was a secondary school teacher, so they had a comfortable income. Both were in excellent health when Bernie got the policy. It was term insurance to age sixty four and not whole life, so the premium was very affordable for them."

"So the term was just about to run out when Ms. Matheson was officially declared dead," Shane commented.

"That's correct," Jason agreed and then said, "The insurance company that issued the policy, Great North, is one of our corporate clients and is prepared to make the payment, but would like us to take one final look at the file."

"Their own investigators have some concerns?" Shane asked.

"Not really," Jason answered. "Great North is a relatively young company and up until this point only uses a part-time investigator who doesn't have a lot of experience. This is the company's first settlement in a missing person's case and they just want to make sure everything has been done properly."

"I'll take a look," Shane said.

"Thanks. Shouldn't take you long to review the file, it all looks pretty straightforward," Jason said.

As Shane stood up to leave the office, Jason said, "Shane, don't forget that if you need time off for whatever, just ask."

"I appreciate that," Shane responded.

After he was back in his office, Shane returned some phone calls and replied to emails that needed an immediate response and then started reading through the Matheson file, concentrating first on the copy of the police report on the investigation into Denise Matheson's disappearance.

It was a weekday morning in July when Denise was reported missing by her husband, Bernie, and Brantford Police, with the help of the Brantford Fire Department, launched an extensive search of the Brant Conservation Area, concentrating on the banks of the Grand River. The Fire Department also launched its boat to search the river, but as darkness fell no trace of Denise was found and the efforts on land and water were called off.

Another search was conducted the next day, including areas further downstream, but by late afternoon both the police officers and firefighters on the scene speculated that if Denise did go into the river and drowned, her body may have gotten tangled in the branches of one of the many trees that had fallen in the river, either because of age or a lightning strike, and had eventually sunk to the bottom.

Tragic for the family that Denise's body was never recovered so they could have a proper funeral, Shane thought as he read through the file. Bernie was asked by investigators if his wife had been depressed or ill prior to her disappearance and he vehemently denied the suggestion she may have committed suicide. He said she was happy and healthy the morning she disappeared and enjoyed going on walks with her dog, Missie, whom she doted on.

After he finished reviewing the file, there were two things about Ms. Matheson's disappearance and suspected drowning that bothered Shane. He was familiar with the stretch of the Grand River that went along the Brant Conservation Area and during the summer months the water was quite shallow along the banks, which meant you had to walk anywhere from five to ten paces out into the river before it started to get very deep. Plus, the current isn't as strong in the summer as it is in the spring when the water is high. If Denise drowned accidentally and didn't commit suicide, why did she walk so far into the river? Bernie was asked by the police if maybe his wife planned to go swimming that morning and was wearing her bathing suit under the shorts and top he saw her wearing that morning. Bernie said no because Denise's bathing suit was still hanging from a clothesline he had tied between a tree and their trailer.

The second thing that bothered Shane was the theory that Denise's dog went into the river, got in trouble, and Denise drowned when she went into the water to try and rescue it. The idea had credibility because the dog went missing at the same time as Denise.

The dog was a two year old Poodle, still young and playful, so it's possible it didn't know any better and ran into the river. But Shane knew two things about Poodles; they're considered one of the smartest breeds of dogs and they're not particularly known for a love of water like a Lab or a Golden Retriever. So even if Denise's dog did like splashing around in the shallow water close to shore, Shane couldn't see it being stupid enough to go out where it's deep and where there's a strong enough current, even in the summer, that it would be very difficult to swim back to the river bank.

It's probably nothing, Shane thought as he closed the file and set it on the side of his desk. Probably overthinking what was a tragic accident, looking for something that's not there. But still, the missing dog bothered him.

Chapter Five

Ivan Barber had been berating himself every day for the past week, often quietly muttering "stupid" to himself.

Ivan was a very worried man, to the point that he had great difficulty sleeping at night and functioning normally during the day, and the reason was entirely his own fault. He had been sloppy, careless and lazy, and possibly ruined the life he had so carefully created for himself.

Ivan had transported the bodies of the woman and her kid into the wooded area of a farm property he remembered Max telling him that he used to own and, once he was there, had found a small clearing where he could bury them and forget they ever existed. But he was already completely exhausted by the time he had carried the bodies, one at a time, from his pickup truck to the clearing, and then walked all the way back to the truck to get his shovel.

Ivan had every intention of digging a hole at least six feet deep and wide enough to accommodate both Iliana and her daughter. Wide enough wasn't a problem because, with his long-handled spade, he had dug up the top foot of an area big enough in about half an hour. He had carefully set aside each section of the rotted leaves covered sod he removed because he planned to put them back on the top of the hole to hide its existence.

But then Ivan ran into a serious problem; the entire top surface of the shallow hole was crisscrossed with roots, big and small, from the mature trees that surrounded the small clearing. He tried to use the tip of the shovel and his weight to cut through the roots so he could dig the hole deeper, but some of them were simply too big around. Ivan realized he would need an pickaxe, which he didn't have, and that meant he would have to drive back to his place to get one and then return. But it was already late in the evening and by the time he got back, he would be working in the dark.

"Fuck!" Ivan exclaimed out loud in frustration. He had absolutely no energy left, his shirt was soaked with sweat that was also running down his face and dripping off his nose, and he was being eaten alive by the cloud of mosquitoes circling his head.

Maybe I could find another spot, Ivan thought, but as he looked at the woods around him in the dwindling light, he knew that wasn't going to happen.

I should have just weighted them down and thrown them in the river, he thought, but he couldn't have done it from shore. He would have needed a boat to take the bodies to one of the deeper sections of the Saugeen, perhaps the area known as the mud flats just outside Paisley.

The river wouldn't have worked, Ivan realized, because there was too great a chance of being seen putting the bodies into the water. The other problem Ivan knew from his experience in his previous life was that bodies dumped in the water, even weighted, don't always stay down.

"Fuck it! I'm too old for this shit," Ivan muttered to himself. I'll just make this work, he thought and threw the shovel aside.

Ivan slid the bodies into the hole, positioned them side-by-side, and noted there was maybe four or five inches of clearance from the top of the bodies to the edge of the hole. It'll have to do, he thought, and then spent half an hour covering the hole, first with loose dirt and then the chunks of sod he had set aside. When he was done, he stomped and jumped on the sod to try and get the area he had dug up as level as possible with the rest of the clearing, but there was still going to be a noticeable hump. He then went into the woods and hauled out fallen tree branches that still had leaves and laid them on top to try and further hide where he had been digging.

By the time Ivan was done, his back and knees hurt, and he was already scratching at the numerous mosquito bites on his face. It was also dark and even with a flashlight, Ivan was concerned he wouldn't be able to find his way out of the woods to where he parked his truck.

He did manage to get back to his pickup that night and now, a week later, he was angry and upset with himself. It took less than three days before some stupid farmer and his dog found the bodies, all because he was too tired and lazy to dig a deep enough hole in the ground.

The discovery of Iliana and her kid was, not unexpectedly, big news in Bruce County, an area of Ontario that recorded very few murders. The daily out of Owen Sound and the weekly newspapers were all running front-page stories about the unidentified woman and young girl found buried in the woods and the television station in Kitchener had a reporter stationed in Paisley doing regular updates. Social media sites were full of comments from people shocked about the murders and speculation from amateur detectives about who the victims were.

Ivan knew there was a chance the bodies would lead back to him and the second he thought that was about to happen, he had to be prepared to flee, either to another part of the country or try and make an illegal entry into the United States. He luckily had documents for other identities stored in the safe in his home office along with a substantial amount of cash.

Despite the potential trouble the discovery of the bodies had brought, Ivan didn't regret strangling Iliana and her noisy kid Rebecca in a fit of anger.

Over the past two years, Iliana had become a lot less subservient, demanding more freedom, and wanted her daughter to be allowed to go to school in town when she was old enough. Ivan kept telling Iliana that none of that was going to happen because it was too dangerous to put Rebecca's false identity into any government system, but she wouldn't listen.

Then late one night after Ivan had consumed half a bottle of vodka, he decided he'd had enough, went into Iliana's bedroom and choked the life out of her. She had woken up in a panic and started thrashing on the bed when Ivan started squeezing her neck, first trying to pull his big, strong hands off her neck and then trying to scratch his face, but to no avail. The kid was a lot easier; Ivan choked her and then jerked his hands quickly to the right, breaking the young girl's neck. There, problems solved, Ivan thought in his drunken state.

Ivan was a bear of a man; six feet tall with thick arms and legs, and a bald head on a wide neck. His eyes were set close together under bushy salt and pepper eyebrows, and his nose was pointed and slightly misshapen, the result of boxing matches when he was a young man. His arms and head were lightly tanned from working in the sun, but Ivan's complexion still managed to look pasty most of the time.

Ivan Barber was sixty eight years old and his real name was Ivanovitch Barbarov. He changed his name shortly after he arrived in Canada from his native Russia with expertly forged documents and two million dollars safely stored in a bank in the Cayman Islands. His friend, Max Ivanov arranged Ivan's purchase of a retiring farmer's large cattle feeder operation on the fourth concession of Elderslie Township, south of the southwestern Ontario village of Paisley.

"You have to basically hide in plain sight," Max told him at the time. "And the best place to do that is in a rural area away from the major urban centres like Toronto."

When Ivan decided to leave Russia, he had achieved the rank of Colonel in the GRU, the Russian military's powerful intelligence service, and was assigned to the Second Directorate, responsible for the GRU's operations in the west. He was supposed to use his position to help advance Russia's intelligence capabilities in the West, specifically the United States, but he worked both sides of the street in order to enrich himself. Ivan had no problem setting up assets to spy on U.S. military operations and then selling out those assets to American intelligence intermediaries for cash. He was also on the payroll of several Oligarchs, the powerful, rich Russians who wanted state and foreign intelligence to further their business interests and to keep up to date on any threats to their position.

As far as Ivan was concerned, Russia was broken, ruled by a despot, its resources being bled dry by a handful of billionaires who continued to get rich while ordinary Russians lived in poverty in a self-destructing economy. Ivan knew that eventually his position would become tenuous, he would fall under suspicion for his activities, and perhaps be arrested. If that happened, he would most certainly be executed. So as soon as he had enough money squirreled away safely out of the country, he would need an exit plan.

Ivan was a young officer in the Russian army and had just been assigned to the GRU when he first met Max Ivanov at a brothel in Moscow they both frequented and where they enjoyed drinks together after each man spent time with one of the girls. After the fall of communism and the collapse of the Soviet Union, Max, who by that time was living in Canada, continued to visit Moscow regularly to further his business interests. Ivan wasn't sure how Max managed to travel in and out of Russia so easily, but he assumed his friend had powerful friends in the government.

The last time Ivan saw Max in Moscow, in late 1990, Max told him he was arranging to take Alina, the young girl he spent the most time with at the brothel, back to Canada with him to be his wife. Ivan figured if Max had the connections to do that, then maybe he would be willing to help him when the time came for him to get out of Russia.

One night when they were having drinks, Ivan got up the nerve to tell Max about his extra-curricular activities and his need to have an escape plan if the GRU found out what he was up to. To Ivan's relief, Max slapped him on the back and said, "Good for you, Ivanovitch! Get what you can because everyone else is helping themselves."

Max gave Ivan the names and contact information of several men who could provide him with documents that would easily pass inspection and arrange transportation out of Russia.

"Come to Canada, my friend! Come to small town Ontario where you can have a peaceful life," Max said. "Buy a farm and get a young girl to look after you, but I must warn you that all of this is going to be very expensive."

"Money will not be a problem," Ivan responded.

For over fifteen years after that conversation, Ivan continued to move up the ranks of the GRU and collect money from anyone willing to pay for intelligence. He lived frugally in a small apartment in Moscow so he wouldn't draw attention by living a lavish lifestyle, but in 2007, at age forty four, he decided he'd had enough and didn't want to push his luck any further.

By that time, Max had been in prison in Canada for over fifteen years, serving a life sentence for murder, but his contacts in Russia were still good and Ivan got his false documents and transportation to Ontario. Not sure where he was going and what he was going to do, Ivan took Max's advice and moved to the same area Max had been living and had talked about during their drinking sessions. He paid over half a million dollars for a working beef feeder operation south of Paisley and moved into the stone brick farmhouse.

Ivan didn't know the first thing about running a beef farm, but he kept the two employees who had worked for the previous owner and put one of them in charge of running the operation. As a former army officer, Ivan knew how to lead men, so that was no problem, and he was a fast learner. His English was good, but Ivan knew his employees were wary of their new boss, this big man with a Russian accent.

It was a lonely life for Ivan, he kept to himself, basically eating, sleeping and working, and very rarely went into town, normally sending one of the farm hands to get supplies. But he was a rich man, the farm was making money, and he was living in a nice country away from the oppressive bureaucracy and villainous Oligarchs of his native Russia.

In 2017, Ivan made the long drive from his farm to the Millhaven Institution near Kingston to see his old drinking buddy, Max Ivanov. He wasn't sure why he suddenly decided to visit Max after so many years, although he had often felt guilty about not going sooner to see the man who helped him set up his escape from Russia, and perhaps he thought it would be nice to see a familiar face from the old country.

When Ivan arrived in the visitor parking lot at Millhaven, he looked at the high walls of the facility, the observation towers and the razor wire, and thought about how intimidating and frightening this place must be for incoming inmates and visiting members of their families. But this is nothing, Ivan thought, compared to Lefortovo prison on the outskirts of Moscow, where many high profile political prisoners and westerners accused of a crime in Russia are taken. Lefortovo had perfected the concept of prisoner isolation, a kind of silent torture.

Once he was through Millhaven's security screening, Ivan was escorted to the visiting room where he sat at a round metal table on a chair that was bolted to the faded linoleum floor. Some prisoners were already at other tables in the large room, many busy talking to women and young children who were sitting across from them.

When Max Ivanov entered the room from a side door, Ivan saw right away how much his old friend had changed over the years. Max used to be like Ivan, physically imposing, but now Ivanov seemed small somehow; thin arms and neck, a pasty complexion, and the thick dark hair that Max once wore proudly was now thin and gray and combed straight back.

"So, Ivanovitch Barbarov has finally decided to come and see the old man!" Max exclaimed with a smile as he sat down across from Ivan. He reached across and shook Ivan's hand and Ivan noted Max still had a very firm grip.

"I'm sorry that you're here and we can't live close together like we planned all those years ago," Ivan said sincerely.

"I made some mistakes and, unfortunately, got outwitted by my brother's son who was fucking my beautiful young wife," Max said with bitterness in his voice.

"You have a brother?" Ivan asked.

"We were separated when we were very young and living at an orphanage in Moscow," Max replied. "He was adopted by a couple in Canada and I was left behind. His name is Ed Daniels and he runs a repair shop in Paisley."

"I know him!" Ivan responded. "My farmhands have taken vehicles to his place for repairs. He's your brother?"

"Yes. He's the reason I chose the middle of nowhere Paisley to live," Max said. "That's where I tracked him down. We became very close, but kept our relationship secret, even from Ed's son. But the son, his name's Shane, is the reason I'm here."

Max made a gesture with his hands and then said, "This is not the time or place to explain the whole thing, Ivanovitch, but back in '91, the kid got nosy and somehow found out my wife's body was buried in the woods of some property I owned."

Max then slapped his hand lightly on the table and said, "But that's all water under the bridge, Ivanovitch, nothing I can do about it now, I want to hear about your life! Tell me everything!"

Ivan spent the next ten minutes telling Max about his farm operation, how proud he was of its success and everything he had learned about the cattle business. When he finished, Max said, "You haven't said anything about a wife and children."

"Well, I haven't really had time for that and I didn't want to draw any attention to myself," Ivan said rather sheepishly.

"What! This is not right, Ivanovitch!" Max exclaimed. "You have money and a successful business and you have no one to share it with and look after your physical needs? You're not getting any younger, you know."

"I keep to myself. I don't know anyone," Ivan said.

"Well, I'm going to fix that, my old friend!" Max declared. "I may be stuck in here, but I've still got lots of contacts. I'm going to make a few calls during my phone times."

"That's not necessary, Max, but thank you," Ivan said.

"Nonsense, Ivanovitch, let me do this for you," Max said and then added, "And I'm wondering if you could do something for me."

"Of course, anything!" Ivan responded.

"Would you go and introduce yourself to my brother?" Max asked. "Make friends with him, if you can? I miss him and there are some things that happened that I know he struggles with. I think he could use some support."

"I will do that for you, Max," Ivan said as he held out his hand for Max to shake.

On a Friday morning, two weeks after his visit to Millhaven, Ivan was standing at the kitchen sink in his house, rinsing his breakfast dishes, and thinking about how he hadn't yet made contact with Ed Daniels as he had promised Max, when a late model, black SUV came up the driveway. Max could see the vehicle through the window over the sink and he watched as it stopped and a young girl got out of the driver's side rear passenger door. She reached back inside the vehicle, brought out a large purse with a strap, which she put over her shoulder, and then a small suitcase, which she set on the ground. After she closed the back door, the driver of the SUV backed out of the driveway and drove away, leaving the young girl standing beside her suitcase and looking at Max in the kitchen window.

What the hell is this? Max thought, as he dried his hand with the dishtowel and walked out of the kitchen to the front door. Once outside, Ivan crossed the narrow porch that ran along the front of the house, went down the steps, and approached the girl. He could see that she was very young and pretty, with green eyes, a petite nose, and shoulder length dark hair. Her mature figure was obvious thanks to a clinging peasant blouse and tight blue jeans.

"Who are you?" Ivan asked.

"I'm Iliana. I've been sent to live with you," the girl answered in well-enunciated English, but her Russian accent was obvious.

Max, Ivan thought, had somehow managed from prison to do what he said he was going to do.

"How old are you? How did you get here?" Ivan asked and then quickly said, "Wait, I don't want to know."

"Does it matter anyway?" Iliana said with a smile.

"Do you have documents?" Ivan asked.

Iliana went into her oversized purse, took out her wallet, removed a birth certificate and a driver's license, and handed them to Ivan. Iliana's photograph was on the driver's license, the name was Elizabeth Rowlands, and it already had the address for Ivan's farm. The birth certificate said Elizabeth was born in Kitchener, Ontario on May 15th, 1999, making the girl standing in front of Ivan twenty one years old, but he doubted she was much more than sixteen.

Ivan knew the driver's license would be a high-end forgery, but the birth certificate would be legitimate, obtained from the government by whatever Russian mobster Max knew in Ontario. Most likely Elizabeth Rowlands was the name of a girl who died shortly after being born and her name was used to obtain a Social Insurance Number. Iliana would have been smuggled into the country from whatever desperately poor part of Russia she came from with the promise of a better life with a rich Canadian. Ivan thought it was sad that young girls from his former country would readily agree to this, but it didn't bother him enough that he was going to send her away, and it didn't bother him at all that he was old enough to be her grandfather.

"So your name now is Elizabeth," Ivan said.

"I prefer my own name. Can I be Iliana when no one else is around?" Iliana asked.

"That's fine, but there are going to be some strict rules if you're going to live here," Ivan said sternly. "First, and foremost, whatever I say goes, no exceptions. You will be responsible for the cooking and cleaning. You will never leave the farm property unless I'm with you and that will likely never happen. You will not fraternize with the farmhands and when you do come in contact with them, you will go by Elizabeth and you will tell them you're my niece who has come to live with me. You understand all of this?"

"Yes," Iliana replied.

"Good," Ivan said, then smiled and added, "And in exchange for this, you will never want for anything and I promise to shower you with expensive gifts!"

Iliana moved in and over the next year, Ivan was never happier. Iliana was a willing lover, never turning down Ivan's advances, and not only did she keep the farmhouse clean and tidy, she also had excellent cooking skills. Iliana explained that both her parents were useless drunks and so she was left with the job of looking after them and her three brothers and sisters.

Iliana learned how to use Ivan's computer and she spent a lot of her spare time on the internet, although Ivan adamantly refused to allow her to set up personal accounts on Facebook, Instagram, TikTok and X, the new name for Twitter. She did a lot of online shopping for clothes, jewelry and electronics, and if she wanted something, Ivan never turned her down. It was his way of keeping her happy while living an isolated life on the farm.

Shortly after Iliana got settled in, Ivan kept his promise to Max and introduced himself to Max's brother Ed Daniels, who seemed very reluctant at first to have anything to do with this big man who said he was an old friend of his brother from back in their days in Russia. Daniels told Ivan that he still kept his relationship with Max secret from his son, Shane, who lived in Brantford and was an Investigator for a law firm. Ivan told Daniels his secret was safe with him and invited Ed out to his place for dinner.

Ed became a regular visitor at Ivan's farm and Ivan was really pleased to see that Ed and Iliana connected right away because he was well aware that he kept Iliana isolated and he thought it was good that she had someone other than himself to talk to. Ivan had decided he would trust Ed because Max trusted him, so he told Ed the truth about who Iliana was. Ed didn't judge and made a point of spending time with Iliana every time he visited the farm, often taking her on long walks around the property.

Everything was going great, as far as Ivan was concerned, until just over a year after she arrived on the farm, Iliana told him at dinner one night that she was pregnant. Ivan reacted angrily, sweeping his right arm across the top of the table sending dishes and glasses flying, many of them smashing into pieces on the floor.

"How could you let this happen!" Ivan screamed at Iliana.

"How could I let this happen!? When I ran out of the birth control pills I brought with me, you refused to let me get a prescription for more! And how many times did you insist on not wearing a condom!" Iliana responded loudly but had a look of fear on her face and tears were running down her face.

"We need to take care of this, I'm too old to be a father!" Ivan exclaimed.

"Please, please, Ivan, don't make me do that!" Iliana pleaded. "I want to have the baby! I get so lonely here by myself! Lots of older men have children and you'll be a great father!"

Despite his cold nature and the indifference drilled into him as a Russian intelligence officer, Ivan had feelings for the beautiful young woman sitting across the table from him, and while his gut told him Iliana and her unborn child needed to disappear, he knew his heart probably wouldn't let him do it.

Ivan was determined to keep his life as private as possible so he hired a midwife from Owen Sound, the only place where they were available, and Iliana gave birth at the farmhouse of a healthy daughter who she named Rebecca because she thought it sounded to her like a good Canadian name. Ivan said he didn't care.

The problems that led to Iliana and her daughter's deaths began shortly after Rebecca was born. The crying and late night feedings drove Ivan crazy and he insisted that Iliana and the baby move to a room he set up in another part of the house. The crying, in particular, irritated Ivan and he was annoyed by the fact the baby cried even harder when he tried to hold it, so he eventually stopped doing it altogether and kept his distance.

Ed Daniels continued to be a regular visitor to the farm, providing moral support when Iliana was pregnant and nervous about being a mother, and after Rebecca was born he brought baby supplies and clothes, which Ivan appreciated, telling Ed he wouldn't know what to get and where to buy it.

But as much as Ivan was, on the surface, thankful for Ed's friendship and support, it deeply annoyed him how close Ed and Iliana had become and, even worse, the fact that Rebecca stopped crying and fussing anytime Ed held her.

By the time Rebecca was two years old, Ivan had reached the point where he had virtually nothing to do with his daughter and was constantly irked by the fact that Iliana spent all of her time with the kid.

He had always been a heavy drinker, but Ivan started to hit the bottle hard every day, not only because he felt burdened by a kid and its now distracted mother, but cattle prices had tanked and he was forced to dip into what was left of his original nest egg to keep the farm afloat. He told Iliana she had to cut back on her online purchases, which had increased substantially because now she was also constantly ordering stuff for Rebecca, who had more than enough clothes and toys as far as Ivan was concerned. Iliana pouted about the reduced spending and didn't speak to Ivan for two days, which added to his growing anger over his domestic situation.

Ivan knew that Iliana had changed from the mild-mannered teenager who had arrived on his farm with her lone suitcase and oversized purse. She had gained a lot of confidence since Rebecca was born and Ivan started blaming Ed Daniels who he believed was putting ideas in Iliana's head. In the fall of last year, Iliana was very upset, but Ivan was secretly glad when he heard that Ed had been arrested for the murder of Max's wife and conspiracy in the murder of his own wife.

Ivan and Iliana started fighting all the time; she complained about his heavy drinking and his foul moods and said he had to allow Rebecca to socialize with other kids and go to school in town. Ivan refused, telling Iliana that her kid would be home-schooled, but Iliana would fight back until Ivan would say he'd had enough and would lock himself in his home office and drink.

Then during one night of heaving drinking, Ivan decided Iliana and her daughter had to go.

Chapter Six

Emma got off the elevator on the children's surgical floor of the Brantford General Hospital and walked toward Lan Pham's room carrying two wrapped packages.

Unlike her first visit with the young girl yesterday when she had just finished a shift at the hospital and was still wearing scrubs, Emma was in jeans and a pale blue, short-sleeved, v-neck top, but did have her hospital security card on a lanyard around her neck.

When she arrived at the nurse's station, Emma looked down the hallway and saw a uniformed female police officer sitting on a chair outside of Lan's room and immediately got concerned.

"What happened? Why is that police officer here?" Emma asked the young nurse sitting facing a computer screen at the desk. Her badge said her name was Jasmine.

"We had some excitement of the wrong kind earlier today and the police decided to post a guard on Lan's room," Jasmine answered.

Jasmine explained that a young Asian man wearing jeans, a t-shirt and a baseball cap arrived on the floor carrying a small bouquet of flowers and went into Lan's room. The nurse at the desk didn't see the man walk past her, but when she looked up from the chart she was working on and saw the man enter Lan's room, she immediately got up to go and speak to him, knowing that efforts were underway to find family or friends of the young girl who lost both her parents in a car accident. Before the nurse got to the room, she heard Lan scream and the man came out of the room, pushed past the nurse, and quickly left the floor through the door to the stairs. The nurse called security but the man managed to leave the hospital.

"Was Lan hurt?" Emma asked with panic in her voice.

"No, but just when she was starting to brighten up a bit and interact with the nurses after your visit yesterday, she's now back to almost a catatonic state, staring straight ahead and refusing to respond to us," Jasmine said.

"Okay, thanks Jasmine, I'll go see her," Emma said and then walked down to the entrance to Lan's room.

The policewoman stood up and Emma held out her security badge, which the officer looked at, nodded at Emma. and then sat back down without saying anything. Emma entered the room and saw that Lan was the same way she was when Emma saw her for the first time yesterday; sitting up in bed with no expression on her face and staring at the wall behind the foot of her bed. Emma felt a wave of sadness but she quickly pushed back the emotion, put a smile on her face, and walked up to the side of the bed.

"Hi, Lan. it's Emma. Do you remember me from yesterday?" Emma asked and then added, "I hear you had a very scary experience this morning."

Lan didn't react at first, just stared straight ahead, but then she slowly turned her head and looked at Emma, who felt her heart break at the sight of this beautiful little girl with a sad face and tears running down her cheeks.

"I'm so sorry that happened," Emma said and suddenly the young girl went up on her knees on the bed, put her good left arm around the back of Emma's neck and started hugging tightly, her tiny body up against Emma's chest. Emma, in response, put her arms around Lan.

They stayed embraced for a long time and nothing was said. Emma could feel the dampness on her shoulder from Lan's tears.

"Everything's going to be okay, Lan, I promise," Emma said softly.

Lan finally loosened her tight hug on Emma, went back to sitting up on the bed, and wiped her tears away on the hospital gown over her left arm.

"It's okay if you don't want to, but can you tell me what happened with the man who came into your room?" Emma asked.

"He was one of the men who looked in the window of our car after we crashed," Lan said as a few tears still made their way down her face. "He told me not to say anything about what I saw going on at our house or he would be back. I got really scared and screamed at him and he left."

"You were very brave," Emma said and reached out and held Lan's hand. Emma took a quick look at the stump on Lan's amputated right arm and noted that it appeared to be healing nicely and was only covered with a light gauze.

"Lan, there is a policewoman just outside your door, so no one can get in here except the doctor and nurses," Emma said. "And I'm going to make sure that you're protected at all times, Okay?"

Lan looked into Emma's eyes and Emma knew the young girl was deciding if she could put her trust in the woman sitting on the edge of her bed.

"Okay, Emma, thank you," Lan finally said.

Emma thought it would be a good idea to change the subject, so she set the two wrapped packages she brought on Lan's lap.

"I brought a couple of things for you," Emma said.

"Can you help me open them?" Lan asked.

Lan worked with her left hand to tear off some of the paper on the two gifts and Emma finished it for her. Inside one box was a Kindle e-reader which got an, "Oh Wow!", from Lan and when she looked in the other box, Emma could tell she didn't know what it was. Emma took the item out of the box, assembled it, and put it on Lan's lap.

"It's to hold your Kindle upright and hands-free on your lap," Emma explained. "That way you only need one hand to swipe the pages."

"Thanks, Emma, I love to read and there's nothing here for me," Lan said and Emma had to stop herself from getting emotional seeing the young girl smile at her for the first time.

"I thought you might be a reader," Emma said. "I didn't know what you would like, so I loaded a few books, but I thought we could look at the Kindle App on my phone and you can pick whatever you want, my treat."

For the next half an hour, Emma and Lan sat beside each other on the hospital bed and viewed books in the children's and young adult section of the App. Emma was surprised at Lan's selections because they were for kids well above Lan's age, a sign to Emma that she was dealing with a very intelligent young girl.

When Emma said it was time for her to go, Lan hugged her tightly again and asked if she could come back.

"Lan, you're going to be seeing me a lot," Emma said with a smile. "I'm going to keep coming to visit you and once your stump has healed and it's time to fit your prosthetic, I'm going to be with you through the whole process."

"Did it take you a long time to learn how to use your false leg?" Lan asked, looking down at Emma's left leg.

Emma pulled up the left leg of her jeans revealing a jointed, metal ankle attached to a prosthetic foot inside her running shoe.

"It took some time and lots of practice, but I can even run with it," Emma said. "You'll see, you'll be able to do a lot of normal things with your new arm."

When Emma left Lan's room, she saw Maggie Sawyer from FACS waiting for her at the nurse's station and noticed that Maggie was somehow wearing even more makeup than the last time she saw her and appeared to have more ear piercings as well.

"Hi Emma, do I dare ask how Lan is after what happened this morning?" Maggie said.

"She's going to be okay, she's a brave little girl," Emma responded. "After some tears and hugs, we had a really good visit."

"That's great news! I'm so glad you've been able to connect with her," Maggie said and then added, "Perhaps we can talk for a few minutes in the same office where we met before."

The two women took the elevator to the ground floor and like the last time they met, they got a coffee at the Tim Hortons kiosk before going to the small office down the hall. After they sat down, Maggie took a file out of the laptop bag she carried over her shoulder.

"I have some more information about Lan's situation I can share with you," Maggie said.

She told Emma that when the Brantford Police found out that Lan and her parents were living in the house with the marijuana extraction lab and they couldn't find any background information on them, they contacted the RCMP. The Mounties suspect the Phams came to Canada from Vietnam through a bogus immigrant sponsorship organization they've had under investigation for over a year.

"To get into Canada, Lan's parents would have paid whatever savings they had and then be indebted for the rest of what they owed," Maggie said. "Most likely living in the house with the lab was part of paying off their debt. They may have been forced to move around to different locations before they came to Brantford."

"Desperate people looking for a fresh start in Canada," Emma commented.

"Exactly," Maggie responded. "Lan was going to school. She completed Grade five at Princess Margaret School. I spoke with the Principal and she called Lan an exceptionally bright student who already spoke excellent English when she arrived at the school and was scheduled to take some advanced classes next year."

"I'm not surprised to hear that," Emma said. "I can tell from talking to her that she's very intelligent and I just found out during my visit with her that she has advanced reading skills."

Maggie shuffled some of the papers in Lan's file, looked at Emma with obvious concern and said, "The thing is, both the local police and the

Mounties are also aware that Lan is smart for her age and they believe she can tell them a lot about the Vietnamese gang that operates the extraction labs and the immigration sponsorship scheme."

"I will not be part of traumatizing that little girl any more than she already has been!" Emma said angrily and then added, "And you shouldn't either! You're supposed to be looking after her welfare!"

"I'm well aware of that, Emma, you don't need to tell me!" Maggie responded with indignation. "I will do whatever it takes to protect Lan and do what's best for her, but she's a material witness to a crime and I cannot stop the cops from talking to her."

"I'm sorry, Maggie," Emma said, softening her tone. "It's just that I've come to care deeply for Lan."

It's even more than that, Emma thought to herself, I've fallen in love with that little girl.

"I understand your anger, Emma," Maggie said. "I appreciate that you care so much."

"So, what happens next?" Emma asked.

"Well, after what happened this morning, police are aware that Lan may be in danger and they've posted an officer outside her room," Maggie said. "But with her arm healing, she can't stay here much longer and I'll have to find a secure facility for her, which we don't have in Brantford, so she'll have to go someplace out of the city."

"I'll take her!" Emma blurted out.

"I can't let you do that, Emma," Maggie stated.

"Why not?" Emma responded. "The people who don't want her to talk won't know where I live. I'm former armed forces and Shane's a former cop, so her safety and security won't be a problem. Lan and I have connected, and she trusts me. If you put her someplace with strangers, I'm positive she'll regress. Plus, when it's time to fit Lan with her prosthetic arm, she will need help adjusting to it, and I have a lot of experience with that."

"I don't know, Emma," Maggie said. "To be frank, you don't have any experience with children, especially an eight year old traumatized girl who has acted out physically toward the nurses. It would be a tough challenge."

"I want to do it and I can do it," Emma said with conviction and then added, "You know it's the right thing to do."

Maggie saw the determination on Emma's face and recognized the look of someone who was now emotionally involved with the troubled young girl in the children's surgical ward.

Maggie smiled at Emma and said, "Okay, I'll talk to my Supervisor and see if I can get it approved. You'll have to agree to a background check and I'll have to do a home visit."

"No problem," Emma said.

After Emma and Maggie made plans for a follow-up meeting, Emma left the hospital and walked toward her SUV in the employee parking lot at the foot of Terrace Hill Street.

I can't believe my feelings about Lan made me make a knee-jerk decision about taking her in without talking to Shane first, Emma thought. He's not going to be happy I did that.

Chapter Seven

Shane had to admit to himself that he was starting to feel a bit stupid, not to mention being bored to the point where he wanted to tear his hair out.

For the better part of a week, Shane had been following Bernie Matheson as he went back and forth to his job, as well as staking out Matheson's house on Maple Avenue, a street lined with mature trees in the central part of Brantford.

He thought it was like watching paint dry. As far as Shane could tell, Matheson led a very quiet life and seldom deviated from his daily pattern; breakfast at 7 am, leave for work by 8, eat the lunch he brought with him at noon at whatever job site he was at, finish work at 4 pm and drive home.

But as he sat in the Charger watching the Matheson home, Shane reminded himself that he was doing his due diligence. Matheson was about to collect a million dollar life insurance policy on his wife who disappeared seven years ago when it was believed that she drowned in the Grand River. The insurance company wanted one final look at the file before it issued the cheque and while Shane could have simply reviewed the police report and the paperwork related to the policy, he didn't work that way. He wanted to have a good understanding of the man who was getting the money and one of the ways to do that was to follow him for a few days, no matter how boring it might be.

Shane had done lots of surveillance work since he joined Burke and Associates, most of it related to people faking medical problems in order to defraud Workers' Compensation or their employer's health coverage provider.

Because he had very little to observe while following Bernie Matheson, it left Shane with a lot of time on his hands to think and recently that was not necessarily a good thing. The death of his father a month ago in a prison hospice still weighed heavily on Shane as he struggled to come to grips with the extremes of emotions he felt about Ed Daniels. There was the deep-seated hate he felt for the man who told him so many lies and conspired with Max Ivanov, an uncle he didn't even know existed, to murder his mother. And then, no matter how hard he tried to deny it, there was grief over the man he had loved and respected so much when he was growing up.

At dinner time on Friday, Matheson finally broke from his normal routine when he walked out of his house carrying a full green garbage bag, which he put in a large, round plastic garbage bin at the curb, got in his car, and drove away. Shane followed him to Fagan's Tavern, a small bar sandwiched between a Dry Cleaner and a Discount Jewellery Outlet in a strip plaza along King George Road. Shane parked the Charger several businesses down from the front of the bar, then walked to Fagan's and went inside.

The interior was dim and it took a moment for Shane's eyes to adjust. There was a bar with stools along one wall and maybe six small round wooden tables with chairs scattered around the rest of the room. Shane spotted Matheson sitting at one of the tables with a man of approximately the same age, a pitcher of beer in front of them. Shane sat on a stool at the corner of the bar near the door and when the bartender came over, ordered a bottle of beer. He watched casually as Matheson and his friend laughed and toasted each other. Shane took his phone out of his pocket, made sure the flash was disabled, held it in front of him with both hands to make it look like he was writing a text, and took several photographs of the two men at the table.

When Shane's beer arrived, he paid for it, took one drink, left the bar and walked back to the Charger. He had an idea and hoped that if he hurried, he could get it done while Matheson and his friend were drinking their pitcher of beer.

Shane drove back to Matheson's house, pulled up in front, and after looking around to make sure no one was looking, he took the bag of garbage out of the bin at the curb and put it in the trunk of the Charger. From there he drove to a nearby small strip plaza containing a variety store, real estate office and a takeout pizza shop, and drove around to the back of the building. Shane figured there would be a large dumpster shared by the businesses, which there was, and he parked the Charger facing the back of the real estate office.

There was nobody around, so Shane got the bag of garbage out of the trunk, walked over to the front of the dumpster, untied the top of the bag and dumped its contents on the pavement. He hoped no one from the real estate office would decide to bring garbage out to the dumpster while he was there and if an employee from either the variety store or the pizza shop came out, he figured they would assume he was one of the real estate agents and he would tell them his garbage bag broke before he got it into the dumpster.

Shane put on some surgical gloves and worked quickly to go through Matheson's garbage because he didn't know how much time he had until Bernie finished drinking beer with his friend and drove home. There was the usual stuff like egg shells, coffee grounds and food scraps, but then Shane got lucky. There was a thick wad of envelopes held together by an elastic band and when Shane leafed through them he realized they were utility bills, credit card statements, and correspondence from the life insurance company Shane was doing the investigation for as well as from another insurance company. Matheson must have thinned out his bill file and thrown out some of the old stuff. This stack of envelopes was going to tell Shane a lot about the man he had been watching.

Shane scooped up as much of the garbage as he could and put it back into the bag, re-tied it, put it back in the trunk of the Charger, and drove back to Matheson's house. Bernie's car wasn't in the driveway, he was still at the bar as Shane had hoped, so he was able to take the garbage bag out of the trunk and put it back in the bin on the curb. From there he drove home.

Shane and Emma lived in a modest bungalow in an older section of east Brantford, the home owned by Emma's parents when they were alive. It originally had old-fashioned pebble-dash outer walls, but Emma had aluminum siding installed and replaced all the windows. When Shane moved in, he and Emma spent countless hours renovating the inside of the house, including expanding the size of the master bedroom and gutting and modernizing the kitchen.

Shane parked the Charger on the street, assuming Emma wasn't home yet and would need the driveway empty so she could park her Jeep in the single car garage. When he first moved in with her, Emma, being the generous person she was, had offered Shane the garage for what she teasingly called "his precious baby", but Shane turned it down, saying the Charger had survived the elements since 1969 and would continue to do so, thank you very much.

Shane checked for mail in the box beside the front door, there was nothing, went inside, poured a can of Sprite into a tall glass filled with ice, and sat at the kitchen table to go through the mail he had retrieved from Bernie Matheson's garbage.

Four of the envelopes contained old credit card statements, two for a Visa and one for a MasterCard, and at the time they were issued three months ago, Matheson had maxed out his credit on both cards. Shane figured that probably hadn't changed between then and now. Another envelope had the sheet a credit card is attached to when you get a new one. It looks like Matheson managed to get a Capital One card with a ten thousand dollar limit, even though a credit check should have shown he was at the debt limit with his existing cards.

It was the last envelope that caught Shane's attention. It was an annual statement from Imperial Insurance for a two hundred fifty thousand dollar term life insurance policy for Denise Matheson. How about that, Shane thought to himself, Bernie had two life insurance policies for his wife, one for a million and this one for two hundred fifty thousand. Shane knew that buying life insurance with different term lengths was known as 'laddering' and the term for this one was age sixty five.

The fact that Matheson had taken out two insurance policies on his wife raised a red flag for Shane and he wondered if the police officers investigating Denise's disappearance seven years ago were aware of it. Money was always a good motive for murder. Even by today's standards, a million dollars, plus another two hundred fifty thousand, was still a lot of money for most people. Was it possible Denise didn't drown in the Grand River by accident, but had some help?

The other thing that bothered Shane was the fact Matheson managed to get both these policies in the first place. Denise was fifty seven years old when she disappeared and age fifty is normally the cut-off age to be able to buy a million dollar insurance policy. Your income, health, profession and any hobby you had that was considered risky were all factors in getting approved. Denise must have passed all that, but still, she was over age fifty. Shane made a note to himself to check on Great North's procedures to see if, as a fairly new company trying to drum up business, they were a lot more flexible than other insurance firms when it came to selling large policies.

And what about Imperial Insurance, Shane wondered, a company he had not heard of. They must have been aware the Mathesons already had a million dollar policy when they sold them one for two hundred fifty thousand. Life insurance companies don't normally allow people to over-insure themselves and stick to the formula of limiting insurance coverage to up to thirty percent of income. Someone at Imperial let this one go through.

But in the end, Shane decided, it didn't really matter what the insurance companies did or didn't do because it wasn't illegal to have more than one insurance policy. If Bernie and Denise Matheson didn't lie on the applications, Denise passed the medical questions, and they didn't miss any premium payments, then both policies are legitimate and will be paid. Bernie got lucky and was about to get one and a quarter million dollars, tax-free.

Shane put the statements back in their envelopes and was putting the elastic around them when he heard Emma coming in the front door.

"Hi! I didn't expect you to be home yet," Emma said as she walked into the kitchen.

"I haven't been here long," Shane said as he smiled.

It didn't matter how long they'd been together, when Shane looked at Emma he couldn't believe his luck to be in a relationship with such a beautiful woman.

Emma walked up to where Shane was sitting at the kitchen table, leaned over, and kissed him passionately.

"Whoa! What was that for?" Shane asked.

"What? I can't give you a romantic kiss?" Emma asked in return. "We haven't spent much time together over the past week and I miss you."

"I do too, for sure," Shane responded and then said, "But Emma, I know you and that kiss tells me that you're up to something that I may or may not necessarily like."

"Your job has made you way too suspicious of people," Emma stated.

Shane smiled and asked, "Emma, come on, what's going on?"

Emma sat in the chair next to Shane, clasped her hands together, and said, "I'm bringing an eight year old girl home to live with us."

"You're what?" Shane asked.

"I'm bringing a young girl who lost her right arm in a car accident that killed her parents to live with us," Emma stated.

And why are you doing that?" Shane asked.

Emma then gave Shane the complete details about Lan Pham's situation, including the threat made by the stranger who got into Lan's hospital room, and her belief that the young girl was too fragile, mentally, to be put in a secure facility out of the city.

"And you decided, without talking to me first, to bring this troubled young girl, who may be in danger, to stay here with us," Shane said flatly.

"I'm so sorry! I know I should have talked to you, but it was a spur of the moment decision," Emma said emotionally. "I didn't think it through, I just knew I had to do something to help that young girl."

"You've become emotionally involved with one of your clients," Shane stated.

"I have, I admit that," Emma said. "Lan is a beautiful young girl, highly intelligent and currently traumatized by the death of her parents, the loss of her arm and the threat she feels if she talks to anyone. She's frightened and very vulnerable emotionally and that's why she acts out."

Emma's news had taken Shane by surprise. Right from the start of their relationship, they had both said they didn't want to have kids. Emma never really said specifically why, other than alluding to a desire to not be tied down by someone or something. It was the same reason she gave for why they never got a dog or cat. Also, at least once a year, Shane asked Emma to marry him and she always joked, "We don't need a piece of paper to confirm we love each other and want to be together. Besides, I don't want anything legal to keep me from kicking you out if you don't fulfil my every desire."

Shane's reasons for not wanting to have children were a lot more complicated. Although he'd had it under control for a long time, Shane had a quick temper, something he inherited from his father, and he worried he wouldn't be a good father because he wouldn't have the patience. And another big part of the reason was because his father and uncle were murderers and liars. What kind of family legacy was that to pass on to a kid?

"You're not saying anything," Emma said, interrupting Shane's thoughts. "Are you angry with me?"

"No, No, not at all," Shane said quickly. "In fact, I was just thinking it's been a while since I let my temper get the better of me."

"It's okay if you're angry with me because I did spring this on you. But you have to tell me how you feel about Lan coming here because I can't do it unless you're completely onside," Emma said.

"Emma, you've always said you didn't want to have kids and now, all of a sudden, you want to look after an eight year old girl. What's changed?" Shane asked.

"I know I've never wanted to make room in my life for children," Emma said. "But I've fallen in love with this little girl who has been left all alone and with a life-changing disability. I'm sorry, Shane, but I have to be there for her."

Shane saw the emotion on Emma's face and he thought his heart was going to break. She's such a strong-willed woman, Shane thought, who always had her shit together, and now this young girl has come along and thrown her for a loop.

"Emma," Shane said as he leaned over and put his hands on top of hers. "If this is what you want, I'll support you one hundred percent. I don't know how much help I'll be, but I'll do whatever I can to help you make Lan feel welcome and supported."

"Thank you, Shane, thanks for understanding," Emma said.

"It's going to cost you several more kisses like the one you gave me when you got home," Shane said with a smile.

"I'll give you a lot more than just kisses," Emma responded.

Chapter Eight

The next day was Saturday and Shane decided he would spend part of it seeing if Bernie Matheson's seemingly mundane life extended into weekends.

In the morning, he parked the Charger up the street from Matheson's house and watched as Bernie, dressed in shorts and an old-style muscle shirt, mowed the lawn. Shane stifled a yawn; he was tired but in a great mood after a night of lovemaking with Emma, her reward for agreeing to let the young girl stay with them. Of course, Shane didn't need the promise of sex to say yes, and Emma knew that.

Still, Shane was worried that he made the right decision to let an eight year old girl into his and Emma's lives. Emma had admitted that bringing Lan to their house might not work because even though she had connected with the young girl, Lan might reject her new surroundings and shut down again mentally. If that happened, Emma said they would have no choice but to take Lan to a secure facility where she could receive help from a child psychologist.

Shane was concerned about the emotional impact on Emma if Lan staying with them was not successful. Emma had come to care deeply about the young girl and Shane didn't want to see his partner hurt if Lan had to go elsewhere. He never thought he would see Emma open up her heart in such a way.

Shane was also concerned about the possible danger Lan would bring with her. He was well aware of how vicious Vietnamese gangs can be and it appears Lan is right in their cross-hairs because of what she might tell authorities about her parent's life in the homes with marijuana extraction labs and the gang members that ran them. Emma had assured him that only Maggie Sawyer and her immediate Supervisor at Family and Children's Services would know where Lan was staying, but Shane was going to do a thorough check on their home security system and, whether Emma liked it or not, he was going to make sure she knew how to get into his locked gun cabinet for the pump shotgun and the small gun safe in the bedroom where he stored his Glock pistol.

After Matheson finished cutting the lawn and cleaning up around the yard, he disappeared inside the house and Shane wondered if that was going to be it for the day and Bernie was planning to spend the rest of this sunny and warm Saturday cooped up in his air-conditioned home, maybe drinking beer and watching the Toronto Blue Jays game on TV. If that was going to be the case, then Shane would head home, where he expected Emma would be with their new young house guest.

However, after about half an hour, Matheson emerged from the house and got into his car in the driveway. He had showered, presumably, and now wore a pale green golf shirt and a pair of cargo shorts. Shane knew that Bernie still kept a trailer at the Brant Conservation Area, the same one he had shared with his wife, and perhaps that was where he was heading to spend the rest of the weekend.

Shane followed Matheson as he drove down the Wayne Gretzky Parkway, got on Highway 403 westbound, exited at Highway 24 and headed south. But instead of turning onto the road to the Conservation Area, Matheson kept going, crossed over Colborne Street west and drove southbound.

Where are you going on a Saturday morning, Bernie? Shane asked himself. There were a couple of places Matheson could be heading along this highway, including the village of Scotland and the town of Simcoe, or he could be headed right to Lake Erie, maybe the tourist town of Port Dover. Shane thought about turning around and heading home and letting Matheson go wherever he was headed, but his curiosity was piqued, so he decided to tag along. Besides, Shane thought, I've spent several days watching this guy do nothing, maybe this will bring something different.

After about half an hour, Matheson entered Simcoe, a quiet town of approximately fourteen thousand residents. He drove through the downtown area and at the town's southern edge turned left on a gravel road and entered what a sign said was the Maplehurst Trailer Park. The Park contained dozens of trailer homes on dirt side streets off the main road, all basically the same shape and size; narrow and long. Most looked like they had been lived in a long time but were well maintained, many with decks and some with screened-in extensions, often called Florida Rooms, the owners added to the front.

As Matheson drove slowly down the main road that separated the park into two sections, Shane pulled over just inside the entrance, realizing that if he went any further it would be obvious to Bernie that he was being followed.

When Matheson turned right onto one of the side lanes, Shane grabbed his cane and a Canon digital camera from its carrying bag sitting on the floor in front of the passenger seat and followed on foot. When he reached the lane Matheson had turned down, Shane stopped in line with the trailer on the corner so there was no chance Bernie would see him in his rear view mirror and waited. When he figured Matheson had enough time to get where he was going, Shane walked around the corner and hid behind a parked van. Matheson had stopped in front of the trailer at the end of the lane, on Shane's left, so he had a good view when he peered around the end of the van.

The owner of the trailer had put down a flagstone walkway from the lane to the steps up to a wooden deck that ran along the entire front of the structure. There was a large, circular flower bed on each side of the walkway, beautifully maintained and a sea of colour from zinnias, petunias and impatiens.

By the time Shane got to the back of the van and had a look, Matheson was already on the deck and the front door of the trailer was opening. A woman walked out and gave Matheson a quick kiss. Bernie has a girlfriend, Shane said to himself. He used the zoom on the camera to get a close-up look at the woman and she appeared to be around

Matheson's age, same height, medium build and attractive, with short blonde hair and perhaps too much makeup for Shane's taste. He took several pictures before the couple went inside the trailer.

Shane made his way back to the Charger and started driving back to Brantford. *I wonder how long Matheson has had a new woman in his life?* Shane asked himself. His wife disappeared more than seven years ago and it's only natural that he might meet someone else to share his time with. *I wonder how long they've been seeing each other?* The suspicious side of Shane wondered if Bernie and the woman in the trailer were perhaps an item before his wife went missing.

After he got back to Brantford, Shane decided to drop by the office just in case Chioma Abiola was there. Chioma was the law firm's researcher but was studying part-time to get her law degree, a life-long goal she had when she emigrated to Canada from Nigeria with her husband and two young children, both grown up now and attending university. Shane respected and admired Chioma for the long hours and hard work she put in balancing family, work and studying, but he had to admit to himself that deep down, he hoped it took her a long, long time to become a lawyer because she was an outstanding researcher and had been a key resource in helping him solve several cases. Chioma always kept her methods for getting information to herself saying legally, Shane wouldn't want to know, but it seemed like there was very little she couldn't find out if asked.

Because it was a Saturday and none of the lawyers would likely be in the office, Shane knew he could park in the small lot behind the building. He entered the code on the keypad and entered through the back door, walked down a short hallway, turned right and then down a row of offices until he reached Chioma's where, as he expected, she was sitting at her desk working on her laptop. Jason Burke allowed Chioma to work flexible days and hours to accommodate the time she needed for her studies.

Shane knocked softly on the open office door and when Chioma looked up, he said, "Working hard on a weekend again, I see."

"Hi Shane, I guess I could say the same for you," Chioma responded. She was a beautiful woman with very dark skin, deep brown eyes and short tight curly hair.

"Just out doing a bit of surveillance work," Shane said as he sat down on the chair facing Chioma's desk. "I'm on my way home but I thought I would stop here first just in case you happened to be in the office and I could ask you for some help."

"Of course, what do you need?" Chioma asked.

"I know I'm asking for a lot, as I always seem to be doing, but is there any way you could find out who these people are?" Shane asked.

He held out his phone so Chioma could see the screen and showed her the pictures he had taken of the man sitting with Bernie Matheson at the bar. He then swiped the screen to show the pictures he had downloaded from his camera of the woman greeting Bernie at her trailer in Simcoe.

"They're related to a case you're working on?" Chioma asked.

Shane explained that he was doing a final look at the disappearance of Denise Matheson over seven years ago before the insurance company paid a million dollars to her husband. He also told Chioma that he had found out that the husband had a second policy on his wife.

"Reading through the police report, there appears to have been no suspicion that Ms. Matheson's disappearance was nothing more than a tragic drowning in the Grand River," Shane said. "But you know me, I'm often looking for things that might not necessarily be there and I am bothered by the fact that Bernie Matheson managed to get two life insurance policies on his wife with substantial payouts."

"And the two people in the pictures you showed me are connected to the husband?" Chioma asked.

"Matheson and the man in the photo met for drinks at Fagan's Tavern on King George Road and they appeared to be good friends, and the woman lives in a trailer park in Simcoe and is probably Matheson's girlfriend," Shane answered. "I know it all seems like pretty normal stuff, but I'm just trying to be thorough."

"Can you tell me anything about the guy in the bar?" Chioma asked.

"I'm not sure, but I think I heard Matheson call him Charlie," Shane replied.

"Well, you know what? Let's try something right away and see if we get lucky," Chioma said and then typed on the keyboard of her laptop.

"Here we go, Fagan's Tavern," Chioma said, then picked up her phone from the top of the desk and dialed a number.

"Hi, I'm so sorry to bother you, but there's been a family emergency and I'm trying to track down my brother," Shane heard Chioma say to whoever answered at the bar. She had made herself sound upset and Shane was impressed with her acting skill.

"I don't think he has his phone turned on," Chioma continued on the phone, "And I know he's a regular at your place and I was wondering if perhaps he was there now. He's an older guy, with short gray hair and wears glasses. His name's Charlie."

Chioma listened for a moment and then said in her emotional voice, "Oh, okay, thank you so much for checking, you have been very kind. Charlie has been estranged from the family and we're desperately trying to track him down. Just so I know we're talking about the same guy, has the Charlie who drinks at your place ever happened to say his last name? He had been using the name Daniels."

Chioma again listened for a moment, picked up a pen, and wrote a name on a piece of paper on her desk.

"That must be him," Chioma said to the person on the other end of the phone. She was silent very briefly, said, "No, no message, thanks again," and disconnected the call.

"I didn't think that would work," Chioma said to Shane with a smile.

"Nice touch with the emotional voice," Shane said and then in a mocking tone asked, "Charlie Daniels?" Was that as in 'The Devil Went Down to Georgia' musician Charlie Daniels?"

"It was the first name that came into my head!" Chioma responded and then asked, "What? A Canadian black woman can't like American southern hillbilly music?"

"Well…I'm…I'm sorry, I didn't mean anything by that," Shane said apologetically.

Chioma burst out laughing and Shane got a very confused look on his face.

"You silly man, I was just kidding," Chioma said when she stopped laughing. "I heard the song playing in the background while I was in a store this morning and that's why the name came to mind. I hate hillbilly music."

"Oh," was all Shane could say, realizing that Chioma had got him good.

"Anyway," Chioma continued, still smiling, "As I said, I didn't think that would work. I took a chance that this Charlie was a regular and that not only would the bartender know him, but she would also know his last name and would give it to me."

"Fagan's Tavern is a really small place, so there's a good chance the bartender would know all of the regulars," Shane said.

"His name is Charlie Upshaw," Chioma said, looking down at the note she had made. "It's an unusual enough name and if he's an area resident, I shouldn't have any problem finding him. I will run him through some of the databases I have access to, including some you don't want to know about."

Since being hired as the researcher at Burke and Associates, Chioma had become incredibly proficient at finding information on the internet and with gaining access to places she shouldn't be. Out of respect, Shane never called her a hacker, but he knew that was exactly what she was, and she was a good one. Chioma figured that if Shane didn't know what she was doing and how she was doing it, then he wouldn't get in trouble if she was ever caught.

"As for Matheson's apparent girlfriend," Chioma continued, "If she owns the trailer, I'll be able to find her through the Town of Simcoe's records."

"That'd be great, thanks Chioma," Shane said as he got up from his chair to leave.

"Is everything okay with you Shane?" Chioma asked.

Shane stopped at the doorway and smiled at Chioma. He knew she was referring to how he was dealing with the recent death of his father and he appreciated that she cared.

"I'm good. I've had some things I needed to work through, but I think I'm moving on from a rather painful part of my life," Shane said. "But on the good news side of the ledger, there's a good chance I can get rid of this."

Shane held up his cane and explained about the advances in knee replacement surgery that would allow him to get one and be able to walk without a limp and constant pain.

"That's wonderful news!" Chioma exclaimed. "I'll keep my fingers crossed for you."

"And what about you, Chioma? Everything okay with you?" Shane asked. He knew she had been very upset when Jason Burke was shot because, like him, she considered Jason to be much more than just their boss. Jason had willingly taken a chance when he hired them and both Shane and Chioma have never forgotten that.

"I'm great!" Chioma replied enthusiastically. "My husband's job is going well for him, although he's not crazy about the daily commute to Hamilton, and both kids are doing well at university. Plus, I'm happy to see Jason back at work. I was really worried about him."

"I know, I was glad to see him back in his office," Shane said and then added just before he walked away, "Maybe I'll see if I can get a Charlie Daniels Band CD for you."

"Don't bother," Chioma deadpanned.

Shane went and sat at the desk in his own office and shuffled through some of the paperwork waiting for him to complete and promised himself he would get to it next week.

While he moved the paper around, he thought about how he might be just spinning his wheels on the Matheson case, looking for things that were simply not there. He did wonder how Bernie, a guy who seldom left his house other than for work and groceries, managed to meet a lady who lived in a trailer park in Simcoe. Is it possible, like he was thinking when the two kissed on the deck of the trailer, that Bernie knew the woman before his wife died? Maybe they were having an affair and made Denise disappear so they could collect the life insurance.

There you go again, Shane thought, being suspicious of people for probably no reason. He blamed his father for it. He grew up believing his father was this stand-up guy whom his wife abandoned, leaving him to raise Shane on his own; a man who loved cars, western movies and trivia, and would do anything for you. Then it turns out he also had some dark secrets, including being a killer. The whole experience left Shane suspicious of everyone, even the people closest to him, including Emma, Jason and Chioma. He felt a lot of guilt about being that way.

But Shane's suspicious mind was working overtime right now and he had a wild thought. He downloaded the photo of the woman in Simcoe from his phone to his office computer and put it up on the monitor on his desk. He then went into the Matheson computer file and found the photographs of his wife. There were only two, one a full-length shot of Denise standing in front of their trailer at the Brant Conservation Area and one was a closeup that looked like it was taken by a professional photographer.

Shane put that photo up on his monitor beside the woman from Simcoe and took a close look. In the picture of Denise in front of her trailer, she was wearing red, knee length shorts and a white t-shirt, and she was overweight. The woman in Simcoe was not and, in fact, had a very nice figure.

The portrait-style photo of Denise showed she had a bit of a double chin, green eyes, brown hair with some gray showing, no makeup, and oversized dark rimmed glasses, probably in style at the time the picture was taken. The woman in Simcoe had blonde hair, an oval face, what appeared in the photo to be blue eyes, no glasses, and makeup, including light red lipstick.

They're opposites, Shane thought, but as he studied the two photos he was sure he saw a resemblance between the two. My imagination? he asked himself. Could they be related? The file said Denise didn't have any siblings. A cousin, perhaps?

Shane decided that the only way to know for sure whether or not there was a connection between the two women was to go back to the Simcoe trailer park and find an excuse to meet with Bernie's friend.

Shane looked at his watch, saw that it was mid-afternoon, and decided he would go home. He shut down his computer and was just about to leave the office when his phone rang. The screen said Ontario Provincial Police, Shane hit the answer icon and said hello.

"Is this Shane Daniels, a former member of the Brantford Police Service and a former resident of Paisley?" a deep male voice asked.

"Yes, it is," Shane answered.

"Mr. Daniels, I'm OPP Detective Sergeant Tyson Cornwell of the Walkerton Detachment. How are you today?" the man on the phone asked.

"I'm fine. How can I help you, Sgt. Cornwell?" Shane responded.

"I'm wondering if I could set up a time to meet with you on Monday," Sgt. Cornwell inquired. "I would drive to your office in Brantford."

"Can I ask what this is about," Shane said. "If you're based in Walkerton, I assume it has something to do with either my friend, Ben Chen, who lives in Paisley, or my late father."

"Due to the nature of what I'd like to discuss with you, I would prefer to wait and tell you when we meet," Cornwell said.

"Okay, that's fine. How about ten o'clock Monday morning," Shane said and then asked, "Do you need directions to my office?"

"No, I have the address and I'll just put it in my GPS," Cornwell replied.

"I'll see you then Sergeant," Shane said and then disconnected the call.

What the hell is this all about? Shane asked himself. I hope Ben's not in trouble again. He and Ben Chen had been friends since they were kids growing up in Paisley and Ben still lived there in his parent's old house. Ben owned a Chinese buffet restaurant in Port Elgin and not long ago, Shane had cleared Ben of a murder charge by finding the real killer.

No matter what this OPP Detective has to tell me on Monday, Shane thought, I'm guessing I'm not going to like it.

Chapter Nine

While Shane was following Bernie Matheson to Simcoe, Emma, with the help of Maggie Sawyer, completed all of the necessary paperwork to have Lan discharged from the hospital and released into Emma's care.

Lan's primary care physician felt the stump on Lan's right arm had healed sufficiently to allow her to leave, knowing that Emma, as a nurse, was well qualified to handle any wound care the young girl required.

Lan was silent and Emma tried not to show how nervous she was as she drove them to her house with a debate raging in her head. *What was I thinking when I decided to do this? What do I know about looking after an eight year old girl? Someone had to do something to help this young girl who lost her parents, but I have absolutely no idea what I'm doing.*

When they reached her house and Emma parked the Jeep in the driveway, she said to Lan in what she hoped was a voice that sounded pleasant and not nervous, "Well, this is it, my home and now yours for a while."

Lan, with no expression on her face, looked briefly at Emma, didn't say anything, then turned back and stared at the house. Emma got out of the vehicle and retrieved a bag from the back containing medical supplies provided by the hospital plus the items Lan had in her room.

She then opened the passenger door and waited patiently, keeping a smile on her face, while it appeared that Lan was deciding whether or not she was going to get out.

A few moments went by, which seemed like an eternity to Emma, and then Lan finally got out of the Jeep. She walked slowly to the front door of the house with Emma following, who then reached out over the young girl's head, unlocked the door, and pushed it open.

"Go on in, Lan, and I'll show you around," Emma said enthusiastically, worried that Lan would refuse to enter the house, but Lan walked in and waited in the small entryway while Emma closed the door and set Lan's hospital bag on the floor.

Lan followed quietly as Emma showed her the kitchen, living room, dining area, and her and Shane's bedroom, and then stopped at a closed door in the hallway and said, "This leads down to the basement where I have my washer and dryer, and where we store stuff, so you won't need to go down there. I saved your room for last."

Emma led the way into the spare bedroom, which she knew, for a young girl, was rather bland with its light gray paint and a few framed landscapes on the walls. There was a dresser and a small vanity with a mirror, both purchased from Ikea when she and Shane redecorated the room shortly after he moved in.

Emma made a trip to the mall earlier in the day where she bought two sets of colourful bed sheets and a light pink comforter with a design involving butterflies. She bought some animal stuffies, including a bear and a horse, and left them on the bed hoping that Lan might like to have them a night. Emma also made the rounds to the various outlets that sold children's clothing and sought a lot of advice from the clerks on what to buy an eight year old girl, including sizes, because Lan was small for her age.

At the end of the day, Emma had two huge bags full of clothes, socks, underwear and other things Lan would need like a toothbrush and toothpaste, washcloths and towels.

The bags were sitting on the double bed when Emma showed Lan her bedroom.

"I know there's not a lot in here right now, but maybe we can work together to brighten it up a bit," Emma said to Lan.

Lan looked around the room and Emma saw that she had tears in her eyes. Suddenly, she walked up to the bed, swept the bags onto the floor, and screamed, "I don't want this room! I don't want to live here! I want my Mom and Dad! And I want my arm back!"

Lan sat on the floor, pulled her knees up to her chest, and sobbed. Emma sat down beside the angry, upset little girl, put her arms around her, and didn't say anything. Tears ran down Emma's face. Look at me, she thought, the tough, former army land mine disposal expert, upset and feeling powerless to help a young girl who has suffered so much.

Emma held Lan in her arms, remaining silent, until Lan had exhausted herself from crying, and then said to her, "I'm so sorry about what has happened to you, Lan, and I would do anything to change it, and I also know that anything I say likely won't make things any better. But I'm here for you and I'm hoping that you'll stay."

Lan, who had been resting her head on the top of her knees, looked up at Emma and wiped the tears from her face with her left arm.

"I'm sorry I got angry, Emma," she said in a soft voice. "I will try to do better."

"It's okay to be sad and upset about losing your parents," Emma said. "I felt the same way when my Mom and Dad died because I loved them very much."

"Did they die in a car accident like mine?" Lan asked.

"No, they died of old age after living a long life, but it still hurt when it happened," Emma replied. She removed her arms from around Lan and then said, "Why don't we go into the kitchen and find a snack? And I know there are two kinds of ice cream in the fridge we can try out."

Over the next hour, after they ate some cheese and crackers, and had a bowl of chocolate ice cream, Emma and Lan went through the bags of new clothes Emma had bought at the mall. Lan seemed a lot happier as she tried on the jeans, shorts and tops, and even giggled a couple of times at the fashion choices Emma had made on her behalf.

"Well, it was just to get you started," Emma said with a smile. "Next time you can go with me and pick out some clothes you like. That's if you'd like to stay."

"I'd like to stay, Emma," Lan answered softly.

They were sitting beside each other on the bed in Lan's room and Emma took Lan's left hand in hers and said, "I meant what I said when I told you I would do everything I can to help and protect you, but I want you to understand there are some things that are going to happen that I will have very little control over. Police officers are going to want to talk to you about the men who came to your house, ask if you heard any names or perhaps have you look at some photographs."

"Like that man who came into my room at the hospital?" Lan asked.

"Yes," Emma replied. "These are very bad people who were likely responsible for forcing your car off the highway and killing your parents. They need to be arrested so they don't try and hurt you again."

"I understand, Emma, I will try, I promise," Lan said.

At that point, they heard the front door open and close, and Emma said, "My partner, Shane, is home. Come and I'll introduce you."

Emma took Lan's hand and led her out of the bedroom, and she could feel the young girl tense up as they walked toward the kitchen. When they got there, Shane had his back turned to them while getting a can of Sprite out of the fridge and when he turned to face them, Emma felt the grip on her hand tighten and Lan stepped back and partially behind her.

"Lan, this is Shane Daniels," Emma said. "Shane, this is Lan Pham."

"Xin Chào, Lan," Shane said, using the common Vietnamese greeting.

Lan didn't reply and Shane could see that she was very wary of him. Lan pulled on Emma's arm so that she would bend down and then whispered in Emma's ear.

"Yes, he is very tall," Emma said in response to Lan's whispered remark. "He was supposedly a big basketball star when he was younger."

"Hey! What do you mean 'supposedly'?" Shane said with a smile, putting fake indignation in his voice. He knelt to face Lan, who continued to hide partially behind Emma and said, "I'm not as scary as I look, Lan, I promise. I'm glad you're here."

When Shane left the kitchen to take a shower and change his clothes, Emma said to Lan, "I know that men are frightening to you right now, but Shane is one of the good guys, like I'm sure your father was."

With a smile on her face, Emma whispered, "Don't tell Shane I said this, but I'm hoping he doesn't make you watch one of his stupid cowboy movies with him."

"He watches a lot of cowboy movies?" Lan asked, appearing to be relaxing now that Shane had left the room.

"That's pretty well all that he watches. It was something he did with his Dad when he was your age," Emma said. "But I'm hoping to talk him into letting us watch 'Elemental'. I hear it's good."

"I've wanted to see that," Lan said with some enthusiasm.

"Okay, that's the plan," Emma said and then she hugged Lan.

During dinner, Lan had very little to say and looked warily at Shane the entire time they were at the table. Emma was pleased that Shane didn't try to push it with Lan and simply smiled at her a few times during the meal. Shane knew he was going to have it take it slow with the traumatized young girl as he watched her struggle to eat with her left hand. Emma had to cut her food for her.

After dinner, Shane helped clean up and then went down to the third bedroom, which he had converted into a home office. Emma and Lan went into the living room and started to watch television, but it wasn't long before Emma saw Lan's eyes growing heavy.

"You've had a very long, busy day. How about we go and get you ready for bed?" Emma said and Lam agreed, getting up immediately from the couch, ready to go.

After Lan had gotten into bed, Emma went to the chair in the corner of the room where Lan had left the clothes she had been wearing and picked them up to take to the laundry room.

"I've installed a night light so it won't be completely dark in your room," Emma said but then realized that Lan was already asleep.

She really was exhausted after such an emotional day, Emma thought, as she went to the bed, leaned over, and kissed Lan gently on the forehead. Her self-doubt returned as she thought about the responsibility she'd taken on and again questioned the ability of someone who had no experience looking after children, let alone an eight year old girl who had lost both her parents and her right arm.

Emma left Lan's room and returned to the living room where Shane was now sitting on the couch flipping through channels on the television. She sat down next to him and Shane muted the TV and put the remote on the side table.

"So much for making a good first impression, she's afraid of me," Shane said.

"I thought you did a good job of balancing between trying to be friendly and giving her some space," Emma said. "Right now, she's afraid of all men and it's going to take time for her to trust you."

"Are we doing the right thing here, Emma?" Shane asked. "Would Lan not have been better off being placed with a Vietnamese family, perhaps more comfortable with people from her own culture."

"That was discussed at length between me and Maggie Sawyer and then Maggie discussed it with her Supervisor at FACS," Emma replied. "But they realized I had established a connection with Lan and felt, at least for now, it was best not to disrupt that by putting her with more strangers. And I did talk to Lan about it and she said she wanted to go with me."

"Don't be angry with me, Emma, but are you sure the personal feelings you've developed for this young girl aren't clouding your judgment over what's best for her?" Shane asked, knowing he would likely upset Emma, but felt it needed to be said. "I mean, as I've said before, what do we really know about looking after a young girl?"

"I'm not angry. Don't think for a minute that I haven't asked myself those questions a hundred times over the past twenty four hours," Emma said with some emotion in her voice.

"But right now," she continued, "given the threat she received at the hospital and my success in breaking through her almost comatose state, I think we're the best option to keep her safe and progressing toward the return to some type of normal life. And hopefully, they'll eventually track down some of Lan's relatives."

"If that's the way you feel, then I fully support you," Shane said and then asked, "I assume the police will want to talk to Lan again?"

Emma explained that through Maggie, a meeting had been set up between her and officers from both the Brantford Police Service and the RCMP to discuss the best way to find out from Lan what information she might have about the people who sponsored her family into Canada and the men who owned the house where she lived.

Emma said she planned to tell them that they needed to give Lan more time to recover from what she'd been through and would suggest that since Lan trusted her, she could ask some preliminary questions and keep notes.

Shane told her not to be surprised if they turned down her request because there would be an urgency to find out what Lan knows so they can act before those involved cover their tracks.

Emma and Shane spent another ten minutes discussing the situation and then Emma said, "Enough about that for now, it's making my head hurt. Tell me what you've been up to."

Shane outlined his work on the Matheson life insurance case and his belief that while on the surface everything seemed to be above board, he had some lingering suspicions around the circumstances of Denise Matheson's disappearance, apparently into the Grand River.

"Your gut instinct about something has never steered you wrong before," Emma said.

Emma's support for his work was really important to Shane and he had come to rely on her intelligence as a sounding board for his theories about a case.

"There is some pressure from the insurance company to get this wrapped up and I understand that Mr. Matheson has been in touch wondering about the delay in his payout now that his wife has been officially declared dead by the court," Shane said. "So, I'm going to have to work quickly. Chioma is doing some research for me and I'll go from there."

"However, the Matheson case is not the interesting news from today," Shane continued.

He then told Emma about the call he got from OPP Detective Tyson Cornwell from the Walkerton Detachment asking for a meeting on Monday.

"What's it about?" Emma asked.

"I don't know, he wouldn't discuss it over the phone," Shane answered.

"Is it possibly about Ben? Has something happened?" Emma said in a worried tone.

"No, I called Ben as soon as I hung up from Sgt. Cornwell's call and everything's fine with him," Shane said and then added, "And you know Ben, he demanded that I let him know what's going on right away."

"That guy needs to get a life outside of his restaurant and his computer," Emma said.

While Emma liked Shane's lifelong friend, Ben's outlandish opinions and his inability to complete a sentence without a foul word in it irked her to no end.

"He's just looking for some drama," Shane said.

"Could it have something to do with your father?" Emma asked.

"That's what I'm thinking, but I can't imagine what," Shane replied. "My father's case was closed a long time ago and he's now dead."

A sense of dread passed through Shane, but he didn't share that he felt that way with Emma, unaware that she was actually feeling the same way

Chapter Ten

To run or not to run, the question had been a broken a record in Ivan Barber's head, but he felt he had finally made a decision.

He knew it didn't help matters that his brain was fogged with alcohol most of the time. I've got to get my head clear, he would tell himself, and then just go ahead and take another swig of vodka.

Ivan was sitting at the kitchen table in his house, the place where he was now spending most of his time, a bottle and glass in front of him, berating himself for the mistakes he made after killing Iliana and her kid. He was a former GRU intelligence officer, the best of the best, but he allowed himself to be lazy and sloppy, and if he wasn't careful now, it was going to cost him everything.

Ivan didn't want to run but he might not have any choice if the discovery of the bodies led back to him. But if he fled, he might end up on the run for the rest of his life or at least constantly looking over his shoulder.

There were also two serious problems if Ivan decided to leave, not the least of which was the money he would need to get settled and live somewhere else.

His investment in the farm would be gone and the bad market had been draining his bank account as he tried to keep up with the farm's expenses. He had always kept fifty thousand dollars in cash in his safe for security, but that, along with what he had in the farm's business account, would only add up to about seventy five thousand and that wasn't going to be enough.

The other problem was identification. If Ivan fled, he could no longer be Ivan Barber and would need a new ID, including a driver's license and credit cards to go along with it. He tried to get in touch with his old contacts, but their phone numbers were no longer in service, the coded emails he sent bounced back, and both the message boards he had access to on the dark web were gone. Ivan had to assume his contacts had either left the country or had been arrested.

It really looked like Ivan was going to have to stay on the farm and hope the investigation went cold because the police wouldn't be able to identify Iliana and her kid. Iliana's prints and DNA won't be in the system anywhere because she was brought into the country illegally from Russia. His DNA wasn't on file anywhere so they won't be able to identify him as the kid's father. He assumed the bodies had been in the shallow grave long enough to deteriorate to the point where photographs of their faces would be useless to check against missing person files or to show around town.

Iliana was never allowed to leave the farm, no matter how many times she begged, which started to happen a lot after Ed Daniels began visiting and whispering in her ear. It got worse after the kid was born, but Ivan steadfastly refused to allow the two of them to go anywhere.

All of the purchases that Iliana made were done online and everything needed for the kid was done the same way.

The midwife that Ivan hired to visit Iliana when she was pregnant, and to help when she gave birth at the house, was from Owen Sound. Both before and after the birth, there were no complications that had the midwife saying Iliana or the baby needed to see a doctor or go to the hospital.

That left the two farmhands, Jack and Mervin, who did have casual contact with Iliana, even though she was told to stay away from them. As far as they knew, the young girl living temporarily with Ivan was his niece, her name was Elizabeth, and she suffered from a type of agoraphobia, which he explained to them was an anxiety disorder that left his niece afraid of leaving the house.

Jack and Mervin lived in a small cottage that the previous owner had built at the back of the property for his employees. They were both single and originally from the east coast and had come to Ontario looking for work, so they had no relatives in the area. They handled the majority of the farm's purchases in Paisley and went into the village on the weekends to drink at the Legion or to attend public functions to meet women.

There was very little Ivan could do at this point but worry about whether the two men ever talked to their drinking buddies or store clerks about the young girl living on the farm, but luckily neither man was very gregarious.

The fact that the two farmhands lived on the farm was the reason Ivan decided, in a rather inebriated state at the time, to transport Iliana and her kid's bodies to what he thought was a remote wooded area instead of burying them on his own property. He was worried that either Jack or Mervin would see him with the bodies or, because the men spent time on almost every area of the farm, they would spot the disrupted ground where Ivan was digging.

Killing the two farmhands was one option that wouldn't bother Ivan, but they would be eventually missed by someone, so that wouldn't work. Instead, Ivan, who belonged to the Grey-Bruce County Cattlemen's Association, sent an email to all of the members he had developed a good relationship with and told them that he had to, unfortunately, lay off two men who were hard workers and good employees. In the email, he said he felt bad about the situation and wondered if anyone was looking for staff. To Ivan's delight, he got a reply right away from a farm owner he knew ran a huge cattle operation near Owen Sound and he said he would hire them right away if they were willing to move.

Ivan brought Jack and Mervin up the house and explained to them that he could no longer afford to pay them and he had to let them go. Jack asked how Ivan was going to be able to run the farm by himself and Ivan made the excuse that because the market was bad, he was going to sell off most of the cattle until things improved.

Jack got a questioning look on his face regarding this strategy but didn't say anything. Ivan handed each man an envelope with cash equal to twice the amount of severance they would be owed and told them about the jobs he had set up for them at the Owen Sound area farm. Both men appeared very happy about the cash and the jobs, they shook Ivan's hand vigorously and headed off to pack.

With the farmhands gone, it left Ivan with the problem of how he was going to run the farm without help. He had no intention of selling off his cattle like he told his now former employees because he would lose a lot of money in the current depressed market. Jack knew this, which is why he got that look on his face when Ivan told him about his plan. Ivan had eighty head of Angus cattle about three months away from being ready to go to auction and an upswing in beef prices was expected, so he needed to keep them in the feedlot.

When he bought the farm, Ivan had sunk a bunch of money into an automated feeding and watering system, which he thought he would be able to maintain on his own in the short term, but he was eventually going to need help with the myriad of other things required to run an operation this size.

For example, Ivan didn't have nearly the amount of expertise that Mervin had in monitoring the health of the herd and keeping detailed records on each steer, a key part of operating a modern day beef farm. Ivan would have to work on his own for an appropriate amount of time so it didn't look suspicious, and then seek two more employees.

Looks like I'm staying, for now, Ivan told himself as he poured more vodka from the bottle into his glass, but he was going to organize a go-bag of essentials just in case he had to leave in a hurry. He would put the bag into the closet at the front door along with a loaded pump shotgun and his Makarov pistol, which he had smuggled into the country.

Chapter Eleven

On Monday morning Shane was in the office early, working on his computer to complete the files he owed some of the firm's lawyers, including surveillance reports and interviews with witnesses for their trials.

He tried to concentrate, but it was difficult not thinking about his meeting this morning with the OPP officer, wondering what it was about. He was also worried about Emma taking on the responsibility of looking after a young girl who was suffering from the loss of her parents and her right arm, and could be in danger from a Vietnamese gang. Shane had full confidence in Emma because she had proven many times that she was tough and smart when it came to dealing with people, both good and bad. But this young girl was a whole different type of challenge.

Last night, he and Emma were jolted awake when Lan started screaming and when they rushed to her room they found her sitting up on her bed, wide-eyed, with tears running down her cheeks. Emma sat on the bed and put her arms around Lan to comfort her, and the young girl whispered something.

"She had a nightmare about the man in her hospital room," Emma said softly to Shane, who was standing at the end of the bed. "I'll stay with her, you go back to bed," Emma said.

When Shane got up in the morning and looked in Lan's room, he saw Emma and Lan cuddled together in the bed, fast asleep. Shane knew he was distracted by the Matheson case and whatever this OPP officer had to say, but he had to make sure he stepped up to the plate and gave Emma as much support as possible.

Shortly after 10 a.m., the receptionist called on Shane's desk phone to tell him his appointment had arrived. Shane walked to the reception area and saw a trim, middle-aged man with brown hair and a moustache, and was wearing a dark suit, a pale blue shirt and no tie. A Glock pistol in a paddle holster was visible on his belt under the right side of his jacket.

Shane introduced himself, Sgt. Tyson Cornwell did the same, they shook hands, and Shane led the way to his office, where the police officer sat in the chair facing the desk.

"Can I get you a coffee?" Shane asked, holding up his mug.

"No thanks. I was working on a large from Tim Horton's most of the way here," Cornwell answered with a smile.

"So, Sergeant Cornwell, my curiosity was piqued all weekend over what you wanted to talk to me about, but didn't want to do it on the phone," Shane said.

"I apologize for making it sound mysterious, but it's a sensitive topic and I didn't think it would have been right doing it on the phone," Cornwell said.

"So what's going on?" Shane asked.

"Recently, two bodies in an advanced state of decomposition were found partially buried in a wooded area just outside of your hometown of Paisley," Cornwell said. "It was, ironically, the same woods where you found your mother's body and quite a few years before that, the body of a young woman."

"And, what, you think there might be a connection?" Shane said and then added, "My mother was murdered by my Uncle, who died in prison some time ago and the young woman, Alina Ivanov, was murdered by my father, who just recently also died in prison. I can't see how they could be connected to these new bodies."

"Let me give you some background," Cornwell said.

The OPP Detective told Shane the bodies were discovered by a retired farmer who lived nearby and was led to the spot by his dog who had apparently already been there several times digging at the shallow ground covering the bodies. The victims were a young woman, approximately twenty years of age, and a young girl, two or three years old. Autopsies revealed they had both been strangled.

"At this point, we have no idea who they are," Cornwell told Shane. "There was no identification with the bodies and the clothes they were wearing are standard brands available at any number of retail stores."

"No one has reported them missing?" Shane asked.

"We went through the missing persons reports for that entire area and there was nothing and then expanded the search to the province-wide missing persons database but there were no matches," Cornwell replied. "Their fingerprints are not on file anywhere. It's possible the woman and the child are from another province and we have people working with the national database, but their bodies were found in an isolated rural woodlot, so we believe the killer was familiar with the area."

"Other than these bodies being found in the same area as my mother and Alina Ivanov, what does this have to do with me?" Shane asked.

"I apologize," Cornwell said. "This has been my roundabout way of telling you that DNA testing confirmed the woman was the mother of the child. We then submitted their DNA to the National DNA Databank and while there was no match for the mother, we did get one for the father of the child. It was Ed Daniels, your father. The little girl was your half-sister."

For a moment, Shane didn't say anything, just stared across his desk at Sgt. Cornwell as the shock of what he just heard went through his body. The coffee in his stomach felt like it had turned to acid.

Shane finally exclaimed. "That can't be true, there has to be some kind of mistake!"

"I'm afraid not," Cornwell responded calmly. "Federal prisoners convicted of certain crimes, including murder, must provide their DNA to the National Databank. The young girl's DNA was matched to

Edward Charles Daniels, now deceased, a former inmate at Millhaven Institute, last permanent address Paisley Ontario. His prison record listed one son, Shane Edward Daniels of Brantford, Ontario."

Shane went silent again, his mind reeling as he tried to accept what he was being told.

"Obviously from your reaction, you were not aware you had a sister," Cornwell said and then added, "I appreciate this has come as a shock, it was the reason I wanted to talk to you in person. I fully understand if you need some time to process the news, so I can leave you alone for a couple of hours, but I'm hoping we can discuss this while I'm here in the city."

"No, No, don't leave, stay, I'll be okay. I do need to discuss this with you," Shane said, mentally taking some deep breaths and trying to calm down.

"So your father never mentioned that he was in a relationship with a young woman?" Cornwell asked.

"No, I had no idea," Shane answered.

Shane told Cornwell that three years ago his father was planning on selling his repair shop in Paisley and retiring, primarily because the decades of working on vehicles had taken its toll physically. They talked on the phone, but at the time Shane was busy trying to establish himself as an investigator at Burke and Associates and was seldom able to drive up to Paisley to see his father in person. After his father was arrested for murder, Shane cut off all contact with him and didn't even attend the sentencing hearing after his father pleaded guilty to avoid a trial.

"Not long ago, I got a call from the prison chaplain telling me my father was dying and that he wanted to see me," Shane said. "I reluctantly agreed and he died a short time later at a prison hospice."

"And during this final visit, he never mentioned that he had been seeing a young woman and that they had a daughter together?" Cornwell asked.

"No, we talked about a lot of things and my father was quite contrite about what he had done and the mistakes he had made, but we didn't discuss what he had been up to in his personal life leading up to his arrest," Shane answered. "There was a time when my father and I were very close and I deeply admired him. I thought we shared everything, but it turned out he had secrets and lied to me about many things. This shock is just something else to add to the list."

Shane shuffled some papers on his desk and avoided eye contact with the police officer as he thought about his father, his murdered mother, and now the murder of a young woman and a sister he'd never get to know.

"What's happening to find out who did this?" Shane then asked.

"We're working under the assumption that the woman and child lived somewhere in the Paisley area," Cornwell said. "Officers have been canvassing residents of the village with a description of the woman and child, as best as we can come up with given the state of decomposition of the bodies, but so far they've turned up nothing."

"The discovery of those bodies would have caused a huge stir in Paisley," Shane said. "It's a small town and the murders would have been, and probably still are, the number one topic of conversation. If anyone knew anything about the woman and her child, it would have gotten around."

"I agree," Cornwell responded. "The people in the Paisley area have always been cooperative with the police and some of the officers stationed at the Walkerton Detachment actually live there, but they've heard nothing."

"So my father met her someplace else," Shane stated.

"Officers are now checking in nearby towns and communities like Walkerton, Mildmay, Chesley, Port Elgin and Hanover but, again, so far nothing about a missing woman and her young daughter," Cornwell said.

Shane told Cornwell that he agreed that the killer was most likely familiar with the Paisley area if he or she knew about the isolated wooded area outside of town. The young woman might not have lived in Paisley, but there was a good chance her killer did.

"I think someone in Paisley knows something," Shane said and then asked, "You said the bodies were in an advanced state of decomposition. What about using facial reconstruction so we know what they looked like?"

"It's been requested, but it will be a long wait before that happens," Cornwell answered. "As you probably know, the reconstruction process takes time and there's currently a huge backlog of cases."

Cornwell then reached into the inside pocket of this suit jacket, took out a business card, set it on the desk and said, "I'm going to head out, but if you have any more questions or if you come up with any information about your father that could help us, please give me a call."

Shane said, "If the woman and her child have not been identified and their bodies are no longer required, I would like to look after the funeral arrangements. It's the least I can do for my sister and her mother."

"I can do that and I'll keep you up to date on the investigation," Cornwell said as he stood up to leave. But before he left the office, he said, "Mr. Daniels, I'm well aware of your reputation and your success in solving several murders. I know you now have a very personal connection to this case, but I must warn you not to consider getting involved. Let us handle it. Your interference would not be welcome."

Shane didn't respond, got up from his chair, walked around his desk, shook Cornwell's hand and said, "Thanks again for driving here and telling me about the murders in person. That was very considerate and if I do come up with any information that will help, I will call."

After escorting Cornwell to the front door, Shane returned to his office, sat at his desk and covered his face with his hands. This is frigging unbelievable, he moaned out loud, took his hands off his face, and leaned back in his chair. My father got a woman more than half his age pregnant, she had the child, and now both the mother and daughter have been murdered.

His father, the man he used to love and trust, had even more secrets than Shane knew about. Ed Daniels had lied to him about so many things but near the end of his life, when Shane finally agreed to see him at Millhaven, he tried to own up to them in an attempt to get forgiveness from Shane. Now it turns out that his father wasn't even close to clearing his conscience.

Why didn't he tell Shane he had been in a relationship with a young woman, that she had a daughter, and that Shane had a half-sister? If no one in Paisley knew anything about this woman and her child, and no one has been reported missing, then where did she live and how did his father meet her? His father didn't like to travel and never left town unless he had to go to a nearby farm to repair a broken down truck or tractor. Did he meet this woman on one of those farms or at a nearby tavern after he finished the repairs? Was it possible the woman was an itinerant prostitute who worked the various bars in the County?

And perhaps the most important question of all was whether or not he should at least give his father the benefit of the doubt and assume he had a one night stand with the woman and had no idea that she got pregnant and had a child.

Shane knew in his heart what he had to do, but it would mean leaving Emma to look after Lan on her own, just when he had promised her, and himself, that he would be there to give her support.

But he had already made up his mind; he was going to try and wrap up the Matheson case quickly and then he was going to Paisley. He had a half-sister he would never get to know because someone had murdered her and her mother. He was going to find out who did it and make them pay.

Chapter Twelve

It was Tuesday morning and Lan was in the living room watching television and Emma was in the kitchen sitting with Maggie Sawyer from FACS, Sergeant Wyatt Lincoln of the Brantford Police Service and Sergeant Gurdeep Singh of the RCMP.

The meeting had been set up to discuss how best to handle any discussions with Lan regarding what she might know about the people who sponsored her family's immigration to Canada and those who ran the resin extraction lab in the house she lived in with her parents.

While they understood the need for the police to talk to Lan and the urgency to do it, both Emma and Maggie had been expressing serious concern about further traumatizing Lan as she tried to deal with the death of her parents and the loss of her right arm.

Emma had suggested that they allow Lan to spend some time with Doctor Charlene Anderson, the highly regarded Psychiatrist Emma volunteered through to counsel newly disabled clients. Dr. Anderson had helped Emma deal with losing her leg to a landmine while a member of the Canadian Forces and eventually they became good friends. Emma and Shane met at one of Charlene's support groups.

Emma tried to concentrate on the discussion around the table regarding Charlene's possible involvement with Lan, but she was worried to distraction about Shane and the shocking news he brought home from his office yesterday. She was stunned when Shane informed her that he had a half-sister who was murdered, along with her mother, and then buried in the same wooded area where his mother and Alina Ivanov were found. After he told her, Emma hugged Shane tightly, felt the tension in his body and silently cursed Ed Daniels for his seemingly endless hurtful impact on his son's life.

"I need to go to Paisley and find who this young woman was, and find who killed her and my sister," Shane had said, looking deeply into Emma's eyes after they had ended their embrace.

"Can't you just let the police handle it?" Emma asked, but she already knew she would just be wasting her breath trying to convince Shane to let that happen.

"I know the area better than the police, I grew up there, and I still know some people who live there," Shane said. "And I've built up some trust, so people are more likely to talk to me rather than the police about what they might know."

Emma was aware that Shane was well known in Paisley, not only because he solved his mother's murder, but not long ago solved the murder of an elderly woman whom his friend, Ben Chen, had originally been accused of.

"I need to do this, Emma," Shane said.

"I know, Shane, I understand," Emma said as she placed her hand on the side of his face.

Shane then said, "I'm sorry because I promised I would be here to help you with Lan, but I need answers."

"It's okay, Shane, really," Emma responded. "Lan and I will be just fine, and I have plenty of resources I can call on if I need help. I'm also going to see if Charlene can step in and help Lan. You go and do what you have to do. When will you leave?"

"As much as I'd like to go right away, I can't," Shane answered. "I need to complete the Matheson investigation. I'm getting pressure from Jason, who is getting pressure from the insurance company because Matheson has contacted them several times wondering when he was going to get his money."

"Have you found anything that would prevent you from signing off on it"? Emma asked.

"Not really, but the circumstances around the wife's disappearance still bother me," Shane said. "Chioma is putting some research together for me and I need to go see a woman in Simcoe."

Emma's conversation with Shane was replaying in her head while the two police officers and Maggie talked about Lan.

"Emma, are you alright?" Maggie suddenly asked and Emma realized that she wasn't paying attention to what was being said at the table while she thought about Shane's situation.

"I'm fine," Emma replied quickly. "Just worried about Lan."

Sgt. Singh of the RCMP then said, "Emma, we're all worried about Lan's welfare. I have two daughters, one about the same age as Lan, so I know how vulnerable Lan is."

Singh was a dark complected man with fine features and along with his black turban, was wearing a dark suit with a white shirt and light blue tie. When he introduced himself, he said he was a fifteen year veteran of the Mounties and had spent the last five in organized crime task forces with various municipal police services across Canada.

"Emma and Maggie, I'm going to tell you some things in confidence so you'll have a better understanding of why it's important that we talk to Lan," Singh said.

The Mountie explained that a large gym bag containing one hundred thousand dollars in cash as well as several suitcases were found in the storage area of the Pham's crumpled vehicle after it was transported from the accident scene on Highway 403 to a police compound. Police believe the Phams had taken the money from the house where they were living and were trying to escape the area when their vehicle was forced off the road.

"It would appear the two men seen at the accident looking inside the Pham vehicle and then leaving were responsible for running it off the highway and were probably trying to retrieve the bag of money," Singh said. "But, unfortunately for them, the car was heavily damaged and even if they did see the bag, there was no way they would've been able to open any of the crushed doors to get inside."

"And they left Lan to die," Emma said.

"Yes, and it's believed that her parents were still alive for a short time after the accident occurred," Sgt. Lincoln of the Brantford Police Service said.

Emma guessed that Lincoln was in his late fifties and he had told them he was a thirty year veteran of the Service. He was thin, it looked like he kept himself in good shape, with a ruddy complexion, blue eyes, a flat boxer's nose, and gray hair cut short.

"If the two men at the accident scene were members of a Vietnamese criminal organization, as we suspect they were, they wouldn't have cared less about the Phams," Singh added.

"If her parents were still alive immediately after the accident, it's possible they said something to Lan or she heard them suffering, which would have added to the trauma she's suffered," Emma said. "Then a man threatens her in her hospital room and it's heartbreaking what she has gone through. Even more reason why she needs time to heal and not be asked to re-live the experiences."

"Has she said anything to you about her home life, where her parents were going the day of the accident, the men she saw at the accident or the man in her room?" Singh asked Emma.

"Very little," Emma answered. "And I haven't asked. So far, I've let her talk only when she wants to and I've concentrated on giving her emotional support. She's been waking up screaming at night. Lan is a very intelligent little girl, smart for her age, and that means she's able to process what's happened and why. But the trouble with that is it makes everything more real for her."

"I understand that, I do, and I'm trying not to be cold-hearted," Singh responded. "But we believe the Vietnamese gang running the house in Brantford is based out of Vaughn, north of Toronto, the same gang that runs the bogus immigration sponsorship program we've been investigating for over a year. We're close to making arrests but are not there yet, and if Lan can provide any information about her entry into Canada or the people who came to her house to run the extraction lab, we can move quickly.

"Timing is critical," Singh continued in a firm voice, "Because we're worried the gang will pull up stakes and disappear. We have surveillance photos of some of the main players in the gang and mug shots of some who have been arrested previously, and if Lan could identify any of them, it would be a huge help."

"Can you give me at least a week with Lan to help her deal with her grief and her trauma? Don't forget, she also lost her right arm," Emma pleaded to the two officers.

"I can try and get you maybe two days," Singh said. "There are officers of a higher rank than me who are running the investigation and they want me to get results as soon as possible. I'm sorry, but I need to talk to Lan, with adult supervision in the room, of course."

Emma didn't say anything for a moment and kept her anger in check because she knew Sgt. Singh was just doing his job. She then asked, "At this point, how much danger do you think Lan may be in from this gang?"

Singh explained that they really didn't know to what extent Lan's parents, Duc and Hai Pham, were involved in the running of the extraction lab in their house. They might have been doing a lot more for the gang than simply making the house look lived in. Singh also said because of the amount of money found in the Pham's vehicle, the Brantford house was also being used as a cash collection point or a transfer station for money on its way to be laundered.

"The visit to her hospital room suggests they're worried about what she saw at the house," Singh said. "It's why we still believe Lan should be staying in a secure facility."

"That would be a mental disaster for her!" Emma exclaimed and then quickly lowered her voice, fearing Lan might hear her in the living room. "No one except for Maggie and her Supervisor knows Lan is here and this house has a high-end security system. She needs to be with someone she knows and trusts."

"Okay," was all Singh said and Sgt. Lincoln just nodded his head.

The two officers left, but Maggie lingered for a moment. She had said very little during the meeting and now told Emma that the police were already well aware of her opinions regarding Lan.

"You did a fine job of standing up for Lan and I felt that if I said too much, it would cause some friction and they would put their foot down and insist on seeing Lan immediately," Maggie said. She then went into the living room and spoke with Lan for a few minutes before leaving.

Emma went into one of the cupboards, got out a container of chocolate chip cookies she had bought at the store, put two of them on a small plate, resisted the urge to take some for herself, and then grabbed a juice box from the fridge. She went into the living room, sat on the couch beside Lan and set the plate on Lan's lap. Lan didn't take her eyes off the television show she was watching as she picked up a cookie from the plate and started eating.

Emma was content to just sit silently beside the young girl she'd developed such deep feelings for when Lan, still looking at the TV, said, "You were talking to those two men about me."

"Yes, they're police officers investigating the accident that killed your parents," Emma said.

"They want to talk to me about what happened, don't they Emma," Lan said, still looking at the TV and nibbling on a cookie.

"Yes, they do, but they also want to ask you some questions about some other things," Emma said.

"What other things?" Lan asked.

"About things that went on at your house and the people that came there sometimes, about the men who looked in the car window at you after the accident, and about the man who came into your room at the hospital," Emma answered.

Lan sat the cookie she was eating on the plate and turned from the TV toward Emma, tears running down her face.

"I will do that, if you want me to, Emma," Lan said.

"Oh, sweetie, you don't have to talk to anyone about what happened if you don't want to, I will make sure of that," Emma said, trying to fight off her own tears because she wanted to make sure she looked strong for this little girl.

"It's okay, Emma, I'll do it," Lan said.

Emma reached over, hugged Lan, and said, "You are a very brave girl."

"When can I go back to school?" Lan suddenly asked. It was early September, the school year was well underway, and Maggie had told Emma that Lan was expected to skip Grade four and enter Grade five instead.

"Soon, I promise," Emma answered, but added, "But first we have to make sure that your arm has completely healed and you're comfortable using your left hand, which I know you're really good at already."

"Do you think I can have some big sheets of paper and some pencils?" Lan asked.

"Of course!" Emma replied. "I actually have an artist's sketchpad because at one time I thought I would like to draw. But guess what happened?"

"What?" Lan asked.

"I found out I couldn't draw. I really sucked!" Emma said with a smile.

That drew giggles from Lan which warmed Emma's heart.

After lunch, Lan disappeared into her room with the sketchpad and artist's pencils Emma had dug out of a storage bin in the basement, and Emma busied herself cleaning out the fridge.

She figured that while she was on a leave of absence from the hospital to look after Lan, it would be a good time to do some of the household chores that there never seemed to be time to get done when you're working full-time. Emma realized she was not what would be considered a good housekeeper and she tended to let a lot of things slip, but was lucky that Shane was just the opposite. He was quite fastidious about dusting and vacuuming, a direct result of being responsible for doing the housework after his mother left and it was just him and his dad living in their house.

At mid-afternoon, Emma knocked on the door of Lan's room to check on her and ask if she wanted a snack. When she opened the door, she found Lan sitting cross-legged on her bed with the sketchpad on her lap, working away with a pencil in her left hand.

"How are you making out trying to draw with your opposite hand?" Emma asked as she approached the bed, not expecting much in the way of results.

Lan turned the sketchpad to face Emma and said, "This is the man who looked in the window of our car and came into my room."

Emma couldn't believe what she was looking at. Lan, forced to use her left hand, had somehow managed to sketch a highly detailed portrait of a young Asian man.

"Oh my God, Lan, that's incredible! How did you do that? And with your left hand!" Emma exclaimed excitedly and then added, "How did you learn to draw like that?"

Lan shrugged her shoulders and said nonchalantly, "My mom was an artist, she showed me. She wanted to sell some of her paintings to get money to help pay our bills."

"This is so impressive, Lan. Do you think I could give this to the police to help them find this man and put him in jail?" Emma asked.

"I don't want it anymore," Lan responded, tore the page out of the sketchpad and handed it to Emma.

Emma wondered if drawing this man was a way Lan was using to deal with her fears and if that was the case, she hoped it was working.

She then asked, "Lan, do you remember what the other man who looked in your car looked like or maybe some of the other men who used to come to your house?"

"Sure, I can draw them for you," Lan said with no emotion in her voice and another shrug of her shoulders and then with sudden excitement asked, "Can I have some more of those cookies, Emma?"

Chapter Thirteen

"A sister? She was your sister! I'm so sorry Shane," Jason Burke said.

Shane was sitting in Jason's office at Burke and Associates and had just informed his boss about his meeting with OPP Sgt. Tyson Cornwell and what the police officer told him about the investigation into the murders of an unidentified woman and her daughter.

"Half-sister, she was my half-sister," Shane corrected Jason.

"I'm sure that doesn't matter to you," Jason responded and then said, "I can't believe this has happened when I know you've been dealing with your father's history and his recent death. Are you going to be okay? What can I do to help?"

The relationship between Jason and Shane had become much more than just employer and employee; they were friends who had developed a deep bond.

"I need some time off to go to Paisley to see if I can find out who this young woman was and who was responsible for her and her child's murder," Shane said in answer to Jason's question.

"That's not a problem, you take all the time you need," Jason said and then asked, "What are the police saying other than I'm sure telling you to stay away?"

Shane outlined what Sgt. Cornwell told him about their efforts to identify the woman, including reviewing missing persons files from across the country and officers canvassing residents in Paisley and other nearby communities.

"I wish my father was still alive so I could find out from him who the woman was and about their relationship," Shane said. "My Uncle, Max Ivanov, was in prison a long time before he died two years ago, but I have a strong feeling he was involved in this somehow. Right from the moment he secretly identified himself to my father as his brother, my father turned into a different person. I think that in many ways, Max was controlling my father and I wonder if his influence continued from his jail cell."

"I have an idea," Jason said. "Why don't I see if I can get my hands on Max's visitor records at Millhaven? It might take a Freedom of Information application or better yet, I have some contacts with the Mounties who should be able to get it. I'll have a document prepared right away for you to sign, making me your legal representative."

"That would be great, thanks," Shane said. "It's possible someone connected to the woman visited Max at Millhaven and then through Max and this person, my father met the woman. It's worth a shot."

"When are you heading to Paisley?" Jason asked.

"I have two things on my plate to deal with before I go, one being the Matheson file," Shane said.

"Don't worry about the Matheson file," Jason said firmly. "Mr. Matheson has been pushing for his payout, which he has a right to, and the company wants to wrap things up. Listen, it was just a last minute due diligence thing and I'm sure you did your usual excellent review, so sign off on it so you can get away."

"Did you know that Matheson had another life insurance policy on his wife worth two hundred fifty thousand?" Shane asked.

"He had a second policy? How did he manage that?" Jason asked, his curiosity suddenly piqued.

Shane told Jason about finding old invoices for the second policy when he went through Matheson's trash, assuring the lawyer that the garbage bin was at the curb so legally it was considered abandoned property. Shane said he suspected that the representative at the second company who sold Matheson the term insurance didn't bother to check to see if Matheson had other policies.

Shane then went on to tell Jason about the woman in the Simcoe trailer park and how he felt there was a resemblance between her and Matheson's late wife.

"Denise didn't have any siblings, but there's enough of a resemblance that she could be a cousin," Shane said. "Bernie doesn't get out much so perhaps he already knew this lady through Denise and they started seeing each other after she disappeared."

Shane hesitated for a moment and then added, "Or the woman in the trailer park is actually Denise Matheson."

Jason got a surprised look on his face and said, "What, you think Denise is still alive?"

"It has never felt right to me that a woman whose husband has taken out a million dollar life insurance policy on, and with no apparent suicidal tendencies, suddenly disappears one morning while out walking her dog," Shane said. "At the time, police suspected Denise and the dog drowned in the Grand River, but the section of the river that goes through the park is slow moving and shallow unless you walk out to the middle. No body was ever found, not even the dog's."

"So you think the Mathesons staged Denise's death to collect the million dollar life insurance policy?" Jason asked.

"And another two hundred fifty grand policy they managed to get," Shane replied and then said, "Or Bernie murdered his wife and her dog and successfully disposed of the bodies, but I've been watching this guy and unless he's an outstanding actor or a psychopath, he doesn't appear to have the demeanour to be a killer."

"Killers come in all shapes, sizes and personalities, Shane, you know that," Jason said and then added, "Not to be hurtful, but think about your father."

"That's true, I was sure wrong about him, plus now I find out he apparently had an affair with a much younger woman," Shane said. "But my gut tells me this isn't a murder, it's a scam."

"Well, we better find out before the insurance company issues the payment," Jason stated.

"I'm going to see Chioma, she's being doing some research for me, and then I'm going to Simcoe to get a close-up look at Bernie's lady friend in the trailer park."

"You said you had two things to deal with before you went to Paisley. What's the other one?" Jason asked.

Shane explained Emma's decision to take in Lan Pham while the young girl recovered from the loss of her arm and to help her deal with the death of her parents. He told Jason about Lan's parent's involvement in a cannabis resin extraction lab in their house and that their deaths may have been the result of them trying to escape with a bag full of money. Shane said that Emma assured him that she would be fine alone with Lan if he went to Paisley, but he wanted to make absolutely sure that was the case.

"I will foot the bill to put twenty-four hour private security at your house while you're away," Jason stated.

"I really appreciate the offer," Shane responded and then said, "But I've been assured that outside of two people at FACS and two cops, no one knows that Lan is at our place. If by chance the Vietnamese gang is still looking for Lan because of what she might know, I don't want to draw any attention to our place by putting a security vehicle out front or even someone in an unmarked car because the gang members would spot it right away."

"If you change your mind or if you talk to Emma and she would like to have it, let me know," Jason said.

"Thanks for the support, Jason, it always means a lot," Shane said.

From Jason's office, Shane went to see Chioma Abiola who was working diligently at the laptop on her desk. After greeting each other and some small talk, mostly a discussion about the weather, which Shane called the national pastime, he filled Chioma in on his theory about the Matheson case.

"So you believe that Denise Matheson and the woman in Simcoe are one and the same, even though they look completely different from each other?" Chioma asked.

"But you have to agree there's a facial resemblance when you put photos of Denise up against the closeup I took of the trailer park lady," Shane said.

"I do agree with that, but Denise was a big woman with dark hair who wore glasses and no makeup, so she would have had to have gone through a significant weight loss and makeover to become the lady in Simcoe," Chioma said.

"I know, but it's possible if you have the right motivation, like one and a quarter million dollars," Shane stated.

"Well, I do have some interesting information for you that will bolster your theory, starting with Bernie's drinking buddy Charlie Upshaw," Chioma said.

Chioma told Shane that finding background on Upshaw wasn't difficult using the various databases she had access to plus public records and social media. She said that Upshaw was fifty seven years old, was on disability and lived in a subsidized apartment in Brantford's Eagle Place area. But the most interesting thing about Upshaw was that he had a criminal record and served time in jail for identity theft.

"Upshaw was originally arrested for several offences," Chioma said. "He was using hidden readers to steal credit card numbers and he had the blanks and the equipment to press cards with the stolen numbers. Upshaw had two accomplices who were stealing wallets and purses, both boys under the age of sixteen, so they were treated as juvenile offenders."

"Upshaw was like Fagin in Oliver Twist," Shane commented.

"I supposed he was," Chioma said and then explained that Upshaw had a process for doctoring the embedded photographs on stolen driver's licenses so someone else could use it for identification.

"Ontario driver's licenses are extremely difficult to forge because of their built-in security and holograms," Chioma told Shane. "But

Upshaw was making micro-thin transparencies of someone else's head shot, putting them over the large and small photos on a stolen license and then re-sealing the card. I was in a file, and don't ask me how I got in because you don't want to know, and I saw a closeup of one of Upshaw's doctored licenses. If you looked closely at it you could tell something had occurred in both the large and small photo areas of the license, but Upshaw was very good at it because the license would pass most quick or casual observation."

"And this is the guy that Mister 'stay at home' Bernie Matheson would meet once a week for a few beers and some laughs," Shane said. "I wonder how they hooked up."

"I didn't go looking for that, but they're both from Brantford and the same age, so it's possible they went to school together," Chioma said.

"So we have Charlie Upshaw, who would know how to build someone a completely new identity using stolen social insurance numbers, driver's licenses, health cards and credit card numbers, and we have Bernie Matheson whose wife disappeared and no body was ever found," Shane said.

"It could be just a coincidence," Chioma suggested.

"Perhaps, we'll see," Shane said and then asked, "What about our woman in the Simcoe trailer park?"

"Her trailer is a rental, owned by Madigan Property Management, which has several units in the Park," Chioma said, "So I thought I wouldn't be able to get a name for you, but then I got lucky because of a mistake someone made."

Chioma said that after she found out that the woman rented and didn't own the trailer, she decided to search the Town of Simcoe records just in case there was some information about the Park tenants. The name of the owner of the Park property, Guild Inc., popped up in the minutes of a Planning Committee meeting where representatives of the company made a presentation on a planned expansion of the Park. The online minutes of the meeting included diagrams from the presentation of both the current Park and the proposed expansion.

"Normally, a line drawing of a property with multiple current units would have each one simply marked as either sold or occupied," Chioma said to Shane. "But for some reason that must breach privacy laws, somebody had pencilled in the names of the tenants of each occupied unit and nobody from the company caught the mistake. So, on the unit your lady lives in, the name is Sally Munsinger."

"Munsinger? Like in Gerda Munsinger?" Shane asked.

"Who?" Chioma asked in return.

"Gerda Munsinger was allegedly a soviet spy who had an affair with a cabinet minister in the Diefenbaker government back in the late 1950s," Shane answered.

"Honestly, Shane, how do you remember stuff like that?" Chioma said, shaking her head with a smile on her face.

"I don't know. I have trouble remembering people's birthdays, but for some reason trivia like that stays in my head," Shane replied.

"Maybe you should try out for Jeopardy on TV," Chioma said.

"I'm afraid I wouldn't last long unless all of the questions were about movie westerns or Canadian history," Shane replied and then said, "Anyway, did you find any information on Sally Munsinger?"

"Nothing for a Sally Munsinger in Simcoe," Chioma answered. "Nothing on social media and in a general Google search. It's an unusual enough name that very few Munsingers pop up on platforms like Facebook, Instagram, TikTok and X, but I did find a Facebook page for a Sally Munsinger in St. George."

St. George was a village north of Brantford that was surrounded by subdivisions of high-end homes.

"I wonder if we contacted Sally in St. George that we would find out she had her purse containing all of her identification stolen sometime prior to eight years ago," Shane mused.

"That's all I have for you right now," Chioma said. "Just let me know if you need anything else."

"Excellent work, as usual," Shane said.

"Thanks, but I lucked out with the names on that planning document," Chioma responded. "I think someone was too lazy to do a new schematic for the Planning Committee presentation so they just grabbed one from the on-site office that was only meant to keep track of who's who in the trailer park."

Shane left Chioma's office and went to his own where he sat and planned his next move. He was having a difficult time not letting the murder of a child who was his half-sister, and his desire to go to Paisley, from dominating his thoughts. Someone who would strangle a young woman is bad enough, but what kind of monster could murder a child?

Shane pushed those questions aside and thought about how he would approach Sally Munsinger, the woman he believed was actually Denise Matheson. The first thing he had to do was find a way to talk to Munsinger, to spend enough time close to her to confirm, one way or the other, that she was Bernie's missing wife. If he was convinced Sally was actually Denise, should he confront her right then and there? Maybe he could do what he's done in previous cases; he could bluff. He could tell Munsinger he had already been in touch with police with proof about her and her husband's fraud and hope that she confessed and didn't ask to see the proof.

Shane decided that either a direct confrontation or bluffing were his two options, but also thought he wouldn't decide which way to go until he got to know Sally Munsinger of the Simcoe trailer park.

Chapter Fourteen

Emma and Lan were sitting at the kitchen table playing various games, currently UNO, and Emma was thinking about how right it felt.

Her decision years ago not to have children was based on a fear of being responsible for another human being and the thought of losing the personal freedom that meant so much to her. But here she was, playing games with an eight year old girl, loving every minute of it, and already dreading the moment when this would be over and Lan would go and live with a long-term foster family.

Shane had shared in the decision not to have a family, but sometimes she felt that perhaps he was just saying that for her. Shane said he was afraid he would be like his father if they had children, that he had some kind of bad gene that would pass a predilection for murder down to their kids. Emma knew that wouldn't happen, but never dissuaded Shane of the notion if it meant he wouldn't try and change her mind about no children. Shane also claimed he agreed with her about not wanting to lose personal freedom, but if that was the case, why on every anniversary of their getting together did he ask her to marry him?

"Emma, it's your turn," Lan said, pulling Emma's attention back to their game.

"Sorry, I kinda got lost in my thoughts," Emma said as she played a card and then picked up another from the deck.

"What were you thinking about?" Lan asked as she put a 'miss your turn' and a 'reverse' card on the discard pile, then held up the card in her hand and said, "UNO!" which you were required to say when you had one card left or you would have to pick up more. Lan had a curved plastic card holder on the table in front of her which allowed her to play one-handed.

"Nothing special," Emma answered and realizing she didn't have a play with the cards in her hand, picked one up from the deck.

Lan immediately put her remaining card down and exclaimed, "I win...Again!"

"You're too good at this game, Miss Lan," Emma said with a smile.

"Were you thinking about me?" Lan said as she gathered up the cards.

This eight year old is so perceptive, Emma thought, and then said, "I was thinking how pleased Sergeant Singh was with the incredible sketches you did of those three men."

And Singh was, in fact, very happy, telling Emma on the phone that Lan's sketches matched both mug shots and surveillance photos of their three suspects in both the immigrant sponsorship scam and the operation of extraction labs operating in houses in several cities. Singh felt they had enough to issue arrest warrants for the trio and then they would have to try and locate them.

"Will you still need Lan?" Emma had asked Singh on the phone.

"I'm afraid so," Singh said. "She will have to give a statement to me and a Crown Prosecutor confirming she did the sketches and who they are. She would do that in the presence of a legal representative appointed on her behalf and a Guardian. We still need to ask her further questions about what she might know and it's possible the court will decide she'll have to testify at a trial if it comes to that."

Emma smiled at Lan while she shuffled the UNO cards for another game and thought about the fact that Lan didn't wake up screaming last night because of another nightmare. That was a good sign, she thought, and perhaps confirmed that when Lan drew the sketches of the three men, it helped her deal with her fears. But would being asked to talk about these men, their visits to her house and their involvement in the accident that killed her parents, cause Lan to regress emotionally and for the nightmares to return?

While Emma dealt out the cards, Lan asked, "I drew those pictures, so do I still have to talk to those policemen who were here?"

"I'm afraid so," Emma answered. "They'll want to ask you some questions about the men in your drawings and if you knew about the bag of money in your car or why your parents had suitcases with them."

"I could tell that my mom and dad were afraid all the time," Lan said. "I could hear them talking about how they were worried about what would happen to us if the men decided to shut down the lab in the basement or if it was discovered by the police."

"They decided to try and get away before that happened," Emma stated.

Lan didn't respond to that and instead asked, "Emma, will you be there when the policemen talk to me?"

"There will be people there to help and support you, but I'm going to demand that I be there too," Emma answered in a firm voice.

"Good," was all Lan said.

That night, after dinner, Shane asked Lan if there was a movie she would like to watch and she asked for 'Harry Potter and the Deadly Hollows-Part Two' because that was the only Harry Potter movie she hadn't seen. She said her parents wouldn't let her watch it because they thought she was too young and it would be too scary for her.

"I tried to tell them I was old enough to watch it and it's not too scary for me because I know it's not real, but they wouldn't listen," Lan said.

Shane looked over the top of Lan's head to Emma sitting on her other side on the sofa and Emma gave a very small nod of her head. Lan continued to be very wary of Shane and he thought this might be an opportunity to help change that.

"I agree with you," Shane said to Lan. "You're old enough and I think you can handle it, no problem."

That pleased Lan who actually smiled at Shane and Emma noticed that she even further warmed up to Shane when she found out, as they watched the movie, that Shane knew all about Harry Potter and the characters in the films. He told her Hagrid was his favourite and she said Hermione Granger.

Shane knew that the two 'Deadly Hollows' movies were the darkest of the Harry Potter films and he watched Lan closely in case the appearance of the evil Lord Voldemort bothered her, but she never flinched, content to munch on the bowl of popcorn Emma had set on her lap.

After they finished the movie and Lan was in bed where she fell asleep quickly, Emma and Shane sat in the kitchen, Emma having a glass of wine and Shane a can of Sprite.

Emma filled Shane in on her latest conversation with Sergeant Singh of the RCMP about Lan's drawings and the real possibility that arrests would soon be made. She also told him about how Lan would still be required to make a statement, identify actual photographs of the men she drew and possibly, down the road, give testimony in a special hearing before a judge.

"If they get these guys, can we assume that Lan will be out of danger?" Shane asked.

"The police are not saying much about it, but you and I both know that if they arrest those three guys, there will still be other members of the gang who may try and silence Lan on their behalf," Emma said. "I don't think we let our guard down just yet."

Emma then asked Shane about his day and Shane filled her in on what Chioma had found out about Bernie Matheson's friend and the woman in Simcoe.

Emma was worried about Shane; he kept her awake tossing and turning in bed and was talking in his sleep. What he was saying was mostly incoherent, but she heard him utter, "Who are you?" several times, as well as, "Max", his uncle's name. Emma knew that Shane was trying hard to concentrate on the Matheson case, but finding out he had a half-sister who was murdered had shaken him to the core and he would have no peace until he had answers about who she was and who had taken her life.

"Shane, I know your focus is on the Matheson case so you can get it completed and head for Paisley, but I thought of something in regards to your father that might help," Emma said.

"Any ideas you have will be a big help," Shane said.

"After your father died, Corrections Canada sent a small box containing the personal items your father had in his cell at Millhaven," Emma said. "When it arrived, you refused to open it and said you were going to just throw it out. Did you get rid of it? Maybe there's something in there that might give you a clue as to who the woman was who had his child."

Emma was right that when the box arrived, Shane couldn't bring himself to look at his father's personal effects and had said he was going to throw the container out, but he changed his mind. He put the box on a shelf in the basement, thinking that the day might come when he wanted to look inside. He had put the existence of the box out of his mind until just now when Emma mentioned it.

"I didn't throw it out, it's in the basement," Shane replied to Emma. "I'll go look just in case you're right and there's something inside that could be helpful."

"Don't do it if it's going to upset you," Emma said. "I can look if you want."

"No, that's fine, I can do it," Shane said.

Very early the next morning, carrying a mug of coffee, Shane went down into the basement, turned on the lights, retrieved the box from a shelf, and set it on the workbench that ran partially along one wall.

The box was sealed with some official looking tape, which Shane cut through with an exacto knife, and he removed the lid. There wasn't as much inside as he expected and guessed his father didn't keep a lot of personal items in his cell or perhaps got rid of some things when he was diagnosed with cancer and was moved to another part of the prison before being transferred to the hospice.

Shane removed a shaver, shaving cream, an unopened package of soap, a toothbrush and toothpaste from the box and set them aside to be thrown out. He then took out three well-worn novels, all Zane Grey westerns, and wondered how many times his father had read them. Like cowboy movies, his father was a huge fan of western novels and Shane figured his father had probably read every one of Zane Grey's books many times over.

There were two faded photographs in the box and a wave of melancholy went through Shane as he looked at them. One was him and his father standing in front of the Dodge Charger on the day his father gave him the car, his sixteenth birthday. The other was Shane in his Niagara University basketball uniform holding his MVP trophy the year the team won the championship.

Next out of the box was a small bible, probably given to his father by the prison Chaplain, and Shane was surprised to see that it was well used. His father was not a spiritual person and often expressed disdain for organized religion. Shane thought perhaps his father found comfort in the bible after he was told he was dying of cancer.

His father's watch and rings were in a small, sealed brown envelope in the box and Shane spent a moment looking them over. One of the rings was his father's wedding band, which his father never took off, even after his mother supposedly left them, but was, in reality, murdered by his Uncle Max. What a hypocrite his father was, Shane thought, for continuing to wear the ring knowing full well he was complicit in his wife's murder. The other ring, a signature type, his father wore on the ring finger on his right hand. The watch was old, but a very expensive brand and Shane recognized it right away because he had given it to his father as a Christmas gift many years ago and remembered how long it had taken him to save up enough money to buy it.

His father's wallet and keys were in the box, which he would have surrendered when he was first arrested and then put in his personal property envelope when he was transferred to Millhaven.

The last item in the box would have also been taken away from his father and Shane was pleased to see it. It was his father's cellphone and Shane thought perhaps it would have something on it about the woman he had a relationship with before he went to prison. It was an older model iPhone and would need a charger cord, but Shane figured he would have something that would work in one of the junk drawers under the workbench where he and Emma kept the cords and outlet cubes from the various iPhones they'd had over the years, and for some reason threw in the drawer instead of in the garbage. After finding a cord that worked, Shane plugged the phone in and while waiting for it to get at least enough charge to open, he started placing his father's items back in the box. He hesitated over the watch and the signet ring, and for a brief moment considered keeping one of them to wear. Why would I do that?, he asked himself, why would I wear a reminder of a man who lied to me about so many things, murdered a young woman and was complicit in the death of my mother? Shane's feelings about his father were a mystery to him and he was always trying to reconcile his current hate for the man with the love and respect he felt when he was a young boy and a teenager. Shane put the watch and the ring back in the box.

Leaving the iPhone plugged in, Shane turned it on and, as he expected, it asked for a pass code. Shane knew this wasn't going to be a problem because he recalled his father constantly complaining about all the user names and PINs he had to remember to get into his computer, his billing program on the laptop at the shop, his online bank account and for his debit and credit cards. Shane remembered telling his father it wasn't a good idea that he kept a list of his various passwords and PINs in a little notebook, but that's exactly what he did. Shane also remembered that, like a lot of people, his father used basically the same PIN for everything, in this case, the month number and last two digits of his date of birth.

Shane put those numbers into the phone and, no surprise, its home screen came up. The first thing he checked was the email and, not surprisingly, the Gmail account had stopped because of inactivity. The last emails his father received were over two years old, mostly junk mail and a series of exchanges with the Legal Aide lawyer he had at the time. Shane scrolled further back looking for any emails that suggested contact of a personal nature with someone who could be a woman, but he didn't see anything. He then looked in the sent items for the same thing, but the only thing he found was a long list of emails that his father had sent to him asking for his forgiveness and begging him to be in contact. Shane opened and read a few of them and then stopped because they were starting to affect him emotionally. He remembered getting the emails and how he had ignored them all.

Shane closed the email program and went to the photo file on the phone and it was there that he found what he was looking for. The last photos taken with the phone, according to the date, were in an album labeled 'Elizabeth' and there were eight of them. All featured a very pretty woman with long dark hair; one with her standing in tall grass in a field with a cloudless blue sky behind her, another had her smiling at the camera while she was sitting in a lawn chair, and two were close-ups. Shane could see how young she was, guessing she was in her late teens, at best.

Shane spent the most time staring at the last two photos and had to make an effort to keep his emotions in check. In one, the woman was standing and holding a baby wrapped in a white and pink receiving blanket and in the other, she was sitting and holding the baby in the crook of her arm so the baby was facing the camera.

This has to be the woman and child found in the shallow grave, Shane thought, because why else would my father have their pictures on his phone? This is the half-sister I will never know. Was the name on the file, Elizabeth, the woman's name? Probably, Shane thought, but maybe his father named the file after the child. Maybe his sister's name was Elizabeth.

Shane felt anger and frustration as he continued to stare at the photos on his father's phone. Why did my father keep something like this secret? When he went to see his terminally ill father at Millhaven, his father expressed shame and remorse for lying about what happened to Shane's mother and for murdering Alina Ivanov. Why didn't he tell Shane that he had fathered a child with a young woman? All those times his father tried to call him from prison and Shane refused to talk to him, was his father going to tell him about the child?

Then Shane's mind went in another direction of possibilities. What if his father didn't know the child was his? What if the woman told him someone else was the father? Maybe the woman was married or had a partner and she let him believe he was the father in order to keep her affair with Shane's father secret. Maybe that's why his father never said anything about having a child and simply felt it wasn't important to tell his son that he had slept with a woman young enough to be his daughter.

Shane knew there was a good chance he would never get the answers to all of his questions, but seeing the pictures of the woman and her child on his father's phone fueled his determination to find out who was responsible for their deaths.

Shane also knew the first thing he should be doing was providing copies of the photos to OPP Detective Tyson Cornwell to aid police in their search for the young woman's identity. He planned to do that, but not until after he was in Paisley and had made some inquiries on his own, and even if that was seen as withholding evidence, he didn't care because he wanted first crack at finding out who the woman was and the person who killed her and his sister.

Shane sent copies of the photographs to his own phone and then to Chioma with a brief explanation of what they were and asked her to make an attempt using her various resources to identify the woman. He then spent some time looking through more of the old emails and the rest of the files on his father's phone in case there was some further information he could use. After finding nothing useful, Shane put the phone and the other items he had removed back into his father's personal effects box and put it back on the shelf where he found it.

Shane could hear the floorboards above his head squeaking, which meant that Emma, and probably Lan, were up and walking around the kitchen. Shane headed for the stairs to go up and join them for breakfast, and after, when Lan was either in her bedroom or in the living watching television, he would tell Emma what he found.

And after that, he was headed for a trailer park in Simcoe.

Chapter Fifteen

Things had gone from bad to worse for Ivan Barber now that the debate he had been having with himself over whether or not to stay or flee had been rendered moot.

Ivan took another pull from the bottle of vodka he held in his right hand and threw another handful of clothes into the large burn barrel he had going in the backyard of the farmhouse. He had been burning Iliana and her kid's stuff for several hours, getting steadily drunker as he did it, sitting in a lawn chair and staring at the flames dancing over the top of the barrel.

Ivan planned to burn all of their clothes, books, bedding and any personal items that could be incinerated. He had smashed the wooden crib the kid had used and the frame of her single bed into pieces, and all of that would go into the burn barrel as well. Ivan had packed the kid's toys, Iliana's jewelry and laptop, and anything else that couldn't be burned, into a large cardboard box which he planned to bury somewhere in the back of his property.

But the task of getting rid of any trace that Iliana and her kid lived with him was not the reason Ivan had started drinking heavily a lot earlier in the day than usual. That was caused by the phone call he received that frightened the hell out of him and confirmed that he had to stay where he was and hope the police never figured out the identities of the bodies he failed to bury properly in the woods and came knocking on his door.

Ivan had tried getting in touch with the people who had supplied him with expertly made false identification when he came to Canada so, if need be, he could flee and start over again someplace else. But his attempts at contact on the dark web message boards and through coded emails came up empty.

However, that changed a couple of hours ago when his phone rang and after he answered, a raspy voice said, "Hello, Chekov," the name that Ivan had used to communicate with whoever it was that got him the forged identity.

"You've been trying to make contact with us," the voice on the phone said.

"Yes, Yes, I have," Ivan said excitedly. "I need a new identity as soon as possible. The price will not be a problem."

"Chekov, listen carefully to me," the man on the phone said, "The only reason you're getting this call is out of respect for the late Max Ivanov who said you were a friend. You fled Russia with a lot of money and normally no one in Moscow would care, but during a recent, uh, I guess you could call what they did to him an interrogation, a man confessed that he had been paying you for information on GRU activities. You've been branded a traitor, Chekov, and there are officials in Moscow who would like to track you down and put a bullet in your head. Do you understand what I'm telling you?"

"I do," Ivan answered, trying to keep the shock he felt out of his voice.

"If we give you a new identity, Moscow will find out about it in a matter of hours," the man on the phone said. "And if they have that, trust me, they will find you no matter where in the world you are."

"I understand," Ivan responded.

"I don't know where you are right now and I don't want to know," the man said. "The original identity I provided you should stand up, but I highly suggest you stay where you are and don't use that identity to travel. As I said, this call was a one-time courtesy. Do not try and contact us again because I guarantee you Moscow will find out."

The caller then disconnected, leaving Ivan standing with his phone to his ear, frozen in place over what he just heard.

And now, several hours later, Ivan sat in his lawn chair throwing clothing and chunks of wood into a burn barrel, taking long pulls from the bottle of vodka, and trying to think if there was some other way he could get his hands on some new identification that Moscow couldn't trace. The problem is he didn't know anybody and wasn't about to start asking around a small town in the highly unlikely chance an identity thief or forger was living there. And even if there was someone, how long would it take before somebody he asked mentioned it to the cops who've been hanging around asking questions about the bodies found in the woods?

Ivan considered the possibility of going back on the dark web, where you can get virtually anything, and searching for a source of documents, but wondered how deeply Moscow had penetrated the web and how many agents did nothing else but monitor it. It was a chance he couldn't take, another reason to sit tight on the farm until the investigation into the identities of the bodies goes cold.

Ivan's thoughts were interrupted by the sound of a vehicle driving up the gravel driveway to the front of the house and as he stood up to go and check it out, he realized he was rather dizzy and unsteady on his feet from the amount of booze he had consumed. While he stood in one spot trying to get his bearings and clear his head, he heard two vehicle doors being closed and a moment later saw his former farmhands, Jack and Mervin walking around the side of the house and toward where he was standing.

"You lads forget something? I thought you'd be at your new jobs by now," Ivan called out, trying not to slur his words.

The two men didn't say anything until they were standing in front of Ivan and then Jack, who Ivan knew always did the talking, said, "No, we didn't forget anything, but we came back because we realized you needed to give us substantially more severance than what you put in our envelopes when we left."

"What are you talking about?" Ivan asked, still working to appear steady on his feet.

"Well, Mr. Barber, here's the thing," Jack said.

Jack was in his mid-forties but looked older because of his leathery, deeply lined face from years of working outside. He wasn't tall, well under six feet, and had a thin, but muscular build. Mervin, on the other hand, was tall and scrawny but did have the same lined face as Jack. Mervin very seldom spoke, leaving all the talking to his friend.

"We hadn't been into town for over a week when you laid us off," Jack continued. "So we decided to stop at a couple of the stores and pick up some supplies we'd need when we got to the new jobs you were nice enough to get for us. The cashier in the grocery store, I think her name's Edith, asked us what we thought about them finding the bodies of a woman and a child in the woods. Did you hear about that Mr. Barber?"

"I may have heard something about that," Ivan answered, keeping his voice neutral.

"I thought you would, considering you had your niece and her daughter living here," Jack said.

When Ivan didn't respond, Jack said, "Anyway, after we got our supplies, Mervin and I decided that before we headed to our new place we would spend a few days hanging around Port Elgin. We started thinking about what a coincidence it was that they found those bodies, and your niece and her daughter, who never left the farm, hadn't been around for a few days when you decided to lay us off."

"Don't try and be coy, Jack, you're not smart enough. Just spit it out, what do you want?" Ivan asked, trying to look calm and sound impatient, but inside he was panicking."

"Well, Mervin and I were thinking that if you gave us substantially bigger severance payments, we wouldn't need to go to the new job, but could head on back to Nova Scotia where no one with questions about the bodies could find us," Jack said.

"When you say bigger severance, how much are you talking about?" Ivan asked.

"I figure fifty thousand each should do it," Jack said.

"A hundred thousand! I don't have that kind of money!" Ivan exclaimed.

"Well, I guess you'll have to find a way to get it," Jack said, crossing his arms for emphasis and then Mervin did the same thing.

"Try and be reasonable, Jack," Ivan stated firmly and then after taking a step closer to the two men, he said, "Look, I'll tell you what I can do. I have ten thousand in cash in the safe in my office, which you can have now, and I can probably raise another fifty thousand, but I would need some time. That would be thirty thousand each. Honestly, it's the best I can do."

Jack didn't say anything for a moment and Ivan figured he was trying to decide whether or not to keep pushing for the hundred thousand. Jack then asked, "When you say you need time to get the rest of the money, how long are you talking about?"

"I need at least a week," Ivan said. "I have to move a few things around and probably re-finance some assets, but I can get you that much money."

Jack again hesitated in answering as he thought it over and Ivan noted that Jack didn't ask Mervin for his opinion. Jack was obviously running things and Mervin was content just standing beside him, staring at Ivan with a stern look on his face.

"Okay, Mr. Barber, here's what's going to happen," Jack said and then quickly added, "I guess I can call you Ivan now that I don't work for you anymore and we're doing business together. Ivan, you're going to go to your safe and get that ten thousand for us. Mervin and I are going to head up to the new farm and start our jobs. One week from now, we'll be back and you better have the rest of our money."

"I'll have it, I guarantee it," Ivan said confidently.

"You better or Mervin and I will tell the cops about your so-called niece and her kid that you kept here on the farm," Jack threatened.

"Wait here and I'll be right back with your money," Ivan said and then quickly turned and started walking toward the house.

Ivan was gambling that Jack wasn't smart enough to go with him to the safe or to send Mervin to do it. Jack didn't say anything as Ivan walked away and he didn't follow him, instead reached into his shirt pocket, pulled out a package of cigarettes, and lit one up.

Ivan went into the house, up the stairs to his home office, opened the small floor safe, removed two of the bundles of cash that were inside and put them in a large business envelope, which he planned to carry just for show.

On the way back outside, Ivan stopped at the closet near the front door, got his Makarov pistol, and stuck it in the top of his pants at the small of his back. When he got close to Jack, he held out the envelope in his left hand and said, "Here you go, ten thousand in cash to start."

Jack took the envelope and with a smile on his face, opened the flap and looked down at the money. Ivan reached behind his back, grabbed the pistol, and then shot Jack in the forehead. He then moved his arm to the right and did the same thing to Mervin. Both men dropped straight to the ground, a large chunk of the back of their heads gone and the ground around them soaked with blood and brain matter.

"Glupyye idioty," Ivan said, calling Jack a stupid idiot in Russian as he returned his pistol to the back of his pants and looked down at the bodies of his former farmhands.

This is a mess, Ivan thought in Russian and then quickly caught himself and repeated it in his head in English. He had trained himself to always think in English to avoid the possibility of contemplating something in Russian and then slipping and saying it out loud in his native language.

Ivan was planning to dig a hole big enough to bury any of Iliana and her kid's belongings that couldn't be burned, but now he faced the miserable task of digging a substantially bigger and deeper one to include two bodies.

I wish I had done that with Iliana and the kid's bodies, Ivan thought, instead of my drunken idea at the time to bury them in the woods. If I had just buried them here on the farm and not worried about whether Jack and Mervin saw me, Ivan thought, then I could have taken my time and not have had to dig in root-infested ground. The bodies would never have been found and I would not be in the situation I'm in now.

Ivan searched through Jack's pockets, found the keys to the Ford F150 the two men had arrived in, and turned the pickup around so the back of the truck faced the two bodies on the ground. I hope I'm strong enough to lift the bodies into the back of their truck, Ivan thought, knowing they would be heavy, otherwise I'll have to roll them onto the loader on the front of the tractor and put them into the truck bed that way.

Ivan was going to use Jack's truck to transport the bodies and the rest of Iliana's stuff to the back of his property, bury them, and then put the truck in the implement shed and cover it with a heavy tarp. He would email the owner of the farm where he had arranged new jobs for Jack and Mervin, and tell him they had changed their minds and had driven back to the east coast.

After that, Ivan planned to open a fresh bottle of vodka, sit in the lawn chair by the barrel in the backyard, burn more of Iliana and the kid's stuff, and try and convince himself that he was going to be okay if he stayed on the farm.

Chapter Sixteen

It was a beautiful day for the drive to Simcoe, the leaves on the trees along the side of the highway were in their colourful fall display of oranges, yellows and browns, and the sumac was a brilliant red.

Shane had to keep easing his foot off the gas pedal to keep the Charger just over the posted speed limit.

The 1969 Dodge Charger was built for speed and Shane liked nothing more than going at full acceleration and shifting through the gears so he could feel the power of the engine vibrate through the steering wheel and see the pavement race under the front of the car.

But it wasn't a good idea to let the Charger do its thing on the two-lane Highway 24 south to Simcoe because it was well patrolled by the OPP and on several previous trips he had passed a radar equipped cruiser sitting at the end of a side road, facing the highway, waiting to nab speeders.

When he arrived at the trailer park, Shane stopped the Charger on the opposite side of the gravel street, one unit up from the trailer he planned to visit. He grabbed his cane from the passenger side of the car, walked the short distance to the trailer, crossed the narrow deck on its front and knocked on the door.

The woman Shane came to visit opened the door only a quarter of the way and asked warily, "Can I help you?"

"Hi, I sure hope so," Shane asked pleasantly. "I'm from out of town and I'm seriously considering buying one of the trailers here in the Park, but I thought I would ask some of the residents first about what it's like living here and if they'd recommend it."

"Well, I love it here. It's a great little community," the woman answered with a smile as she opened the door the rest of the way.

"I'm glad to hear that," Shane said and then added, "I'm so sorry to bother you, but I have a few other questions about the Park if you don't mind.

"Not at all!" the woman answered enthusiastically. "Would you like to come in and see the inside? I can make some coffee."

"I would love a coffee," Shane responded. "I'm Shane Daniels, by the way."

"I'm Sally Munsinger, nice to meet you, come on in," Sally said and then turned and led the way inside to the trailer's kitchen.

From the moment Sally had opened the door, Shane had been appraising her very carefully. Now that he was up close, he could see her strong resemblance to Denise Matheson, but there were some significant differences, not the least of which was their build. Sally was the same height as Denise, but Denise was a heavy-set woman, overweight, with a bit of a double chin. The woman who answered the door was of medium build, with a noticeably nice figure in tight, knee-length blue shorts and a light pink, v-neck t-shirt over sizeable breasts, something the photographs of Denise showed she didn't have. Denise had stringy dark hair, and brown eyes, wore glasses and no makeup. Sally had shoulder-length blonde hair, Shane couldn't see any dark roots, blue eyes, no glasses and expertly applied makeup, including eyeliner and shadow, and light red lipstick. A good looking woman, Shane thought, but the resemblance was definitely there unless he was just seeing what he wanted to see.

Shane sat at the small round table in the trailer's kitchen while Sally started organizing the coffeemaker. He saw there was a pair of wire-rimmed glasses sitting on the counter.

"How long have you lived here?" Shane asked.

Sally turned around from the coffeemaker to face Shane and answered, "It's coming up to eight years, so I'm one of the old-timers around here."

"Well, it must be a nice place if you've lived here that long," Shane said and then asked, "Do you mind if I use your bathroom?"

"Of course not, it's down the hallway on the right," Sally answered and turned back to resume filling the coffeemaker.

Shane grabbed his cane, got up from the table, and walked down the hallway, taking a quick glance over his shoulder to make sure that where Sally was standing in the kitchen put her out of sight.

He stopped at an open door on his left, saw that it was the bedroom, ducked inside and took a look around. When Shane had entered the trailer, he noticed there were no framed photographs in the living room area to his right and now he didn't see any in the bedroom either. There was another pair of glasses, dark-rimmed this time, sitting beside a paperback novel on the nightstand. There was a tall dresser with five drawers and Shane started rapidly opening and closing each one so he could have a quick look, but stopped at the fourth drawer because inside were two very thickly padded bras. That would explain the breasts, he thought.

Shane went to the bedroom door, took a quick peek down the hallway to make sure Sally was still out of sight, and then walked into the bathroom opposite and closed the door. He opened the mirrored medicine cabinet and saw most of the things you would expect to find, like a box of bandaids, headache tablets and toothpaste, but he also found a box of disposable contact lenses that made your eyes look blue, which is why Sally didn't have Denise's brown eyes. Also in the cabinet was a prescription bottle of Rybelsus, which Shane knew was the pill form of Ozempic, a medication for diabetics, which had become very popular for weight loss. There was also a bottle of something called Zantrex, described on the label as a rapid weight loss and energy support pill. There were no hair colouring products, but that just meant it was done at a salon.

Shane had to admit he was impressed by the incredible amount of determination and discipline it took for Denise Matheson to turn herself into Sally Munsinger and live an alternate life for eight years so she and Bernie could get the big life insurance payout.

Shane flushed the toilet, left the bathroom, and walked back to the kitchen where Sally was sitting at the table, a mug of coffee in front of her and another mug waiting for Shane. He sat down and smiled at the woman across the table and tried to decide the best way to break the news to her that her scam was over and there was jail, not a million dollars, in her future.

Shane was just about to say something when he heard clicking noises, looked down, and realized it was the sound of the nails on the paws of a small poodle as it walked across the kitchen floor tile.

"There you are!" Sally, who Shane was now thinking of as Denise, said to the dog. "You've been sleeping on the chair the whole time we've had company."

Denise leaned over, picked up the poodle, put it on her lap, and while she stroked its head, said to Shane, "This is Missie. She's not a spring chicken anymore, so she walks slowly and sleeps most of the day."

"How old is Missie?" Shane asked, although he already had a pretty good idea.

"She's ten, but is still fairly healthy for her age," Denise answered and then kissed the small circle of curly fur on the top of the dog's head.

"It was a mistake keeping the dog, Denise," Shane said.

"Pardon me?" Denise asked.

"When you staged your disappearance in Brant Park over seven years ago, your two year old poodle supposedly drowned in the river with you," Shane said. "But when you became Sally Munsinger, you couldn't bring yourself to give up the dog and that was a mistake."

"I have no idea what you're talking about!" Denise said loudly, but Shane could see the signs of panic on her face.

"You can lose a lot of weight and completely change your appearance, which you did an excellent job of doing by the way, and you can fool a lot of people, including almost me, but there's very little you can do to disguise your dog, other than a different hair cut," Shane said. "How long do you think it would take me, or the police, to track down your previous Veterinarian in Brantford and get a look at Missie's old file, which shouldn't be confidential since she's supposed to be dead. Wouldn't take much to identify Missie using that file. Who knows, maybe Missie even has a chip."

"Who the hell are you!?" Denise said angrily as she suddenly stood up and the dog dropped to the floor.

Shane ignored the question and said, "Of course, the dog who's supposed to be dead is one thing, but we'd still have to confirm your identity, which shouldn't be a problem. I'm sure Bernie will still have something of yours at the house with DNA to match with your mouth swab."

"I don't know who you are and what you're after, but I want you out of my trailer right now!" Denise yelled as she pointed toward the front door. Her face had gone red from both anger and from what Shane believed to be panic over the realization she had been caught.

"Denise, I'm working with the life insurance company that was just about to pay your husband a million dollars, but that's not going to happen now because your scam is over," Shane said. "And you can forget about the other two hundred fifty thousand you planned to rip off from another unsuspecting company."

"Get out! Get out!" Denise screamed and the dog started barking.

Shane left the trailer, walked to where he parked the Charger, got in and then waited.

Less than fifteen minutes later, he watched as Denise left the trailer with an oversized handbag over her shoulder and pulling a large roll-along suitcase. While she loaded the two items into the back of a compact Hyundai that was parked outside the trailer, Shane called 911 and reported that he was watching a crime in progress, gave the address, and said the police had to hurry. When the dispatcher asked Shane for his name, he said, "Just hurry," then hung up.

The OPP handled policing in the Simcoe area, but unless a cruiser happened to be in town, it was going to take some time for an officer to arrive at the trailer park.

Shane watched as Denise went back inside the trailer and a few minutes later emerged pulling another suitcase and carrying the poodle with one arm. After the suitcase was in the trunk and the dog in the back seat, Denise got behind the wheel of her car, ready to leave. There was no sign of the cops yet and Shane didn't want Denise leaving the area and disappearing again, so he started up the Charger and pulled it across the street, blocking it.

Denise moved her car a few feet, stopped, got out and standing behind the open driver's door she yelled at Shane, "Move your God damn car! You have no authority to block the road and keep me from leaving!"

Shane got out of the Charger and because he was tall, he could see Denise over the roof of his car. "Come on, Denise, you know your scam is over," Shane called over. "Just stay where you are until the police arrive. There's no sense running because the police will just arrest Bernie and he'll take the fall for everything. I'm sure you don't want that."

Denise didn't respond to what Shane said and instead yelled, "If you don't move your car, I'm going to smash it out of the way!"

"Really, Denise? With a tin can Hyundai?" Shane said, but he watched as Denise got back in her car and started revving the engine, her hands gripping the top of the steering wheel, glaring fiercely at him, hoping that would frighten him into backing the Charger out of the way.

Shane heard the crunching of tires on the gravel street as a car approached behind him and when he glanced over his shoulder he saw that it was an OPP cruiser heading his way. He then yelled over at Denise, "Okay, you win, don't smash my car, I'm going to move it!"

Shane got in the Charger and couldn't help but smile as he reversed and turned so the car was back on the side of the road. Denise immediately moved forward, but instead of leaving the trailer park, she came bumper to bumper with the OPP cruiser.

Chapter Seventeen

The next morning, Shane was making good time as he travelled northwest along the Elora Road on his way to his hometown of Paisley and hopefully some answers about the murders of a young woman and her young daughter, his half-sister. He stifled a yawn and acknowledged to himself that he was still tired after what turned out to be a very long day yesterday.

After Denise Matheson realized that her attempt to drive out of the trailer park and escape the area was blocked by an OPP cruiser, she tried a new strategy by quickly exiting her car, running up to the driver's side of the cruiser, and with a look of fear on her face, yelled at the officer inside, "Thank God you're here!" pointed at Shane and continued, "That man is harassing me! He's preventing me from leaving the park! I'm in fear for my life!"

The OPP officer, a tall, well-built, middle-aged man, got quickly out of his cruiser, stepped close to Denise, looked over at Shane, who was standing beside the Charger, and exclaimed, "Sir, you stay right where you are!"

As he walked toward him, Shane could see the officer reaching for the handcuffs in a pouch on his utility belt so he said, "This is not what it looks like. I was the one who called the police and if you give me at least thirty seconds I can explain what's actually going on."

The officer didn't accept that, put Shane in handcuffs anyway, and sat him in the back of the cruiser. Before he closed the door, Shane tried again to get the officer to allow him to speak, but the Constable held up his hand and said, "I'll get to you, sir, but first I'm going to speak to the lady about what has happened here."

Shane watched through the passenger window of the cruiser as Denise spoke animatedly to the officer, waving her arms and occasionally pointing his way. While she was doing that, another cruiser arrived and parked behind the first one. A Constable got out and joined his colleague, but by this time Denise was walking back to her car and Shawn suspected she had told the officer she wanted to leave. Thankfully, he shook his head at her and the other officer took Denise and put her in the back of his cruiser. She's bold, I'll give her that, Shane thought.

What followed for Shane was over four hours of often intense discussions with various police officers, eventually ending after he met with Detectives with the OPP fraud squad. There were background checks, written statements, several calls back and forth between Shane, police officers and Jason Burke, and eventually an appearance by the lawyer at the OPP Detachment in Simcoe.

Late in the day, Shane was finally allowed to go home and Denise was in custody, charged with fraud, conspiracy to commit fraud and impersonation, but more charges were expected. Officers were sent to arrest Bernie.

Shane followed Jason back to Brantford and they met in Jason's office where Shane briefed him on how he had arrived at the fact that Denise was still alive and living in Simcoe under a false name, giving Chioma a lot of credit for making it happen.

"I thought this would be just a routine final check," Jason said, shaking his head. "Thanks to you, our client is going to save a million dollars, and if Bernie and Denise plead guilty and there's no trial, they'll save hundreds of thousands of dollars in legal fees. And you can bet that I'm going to inform the other life insurance company that we just saved them two hundred fifty thousand. Your gut instinct turned out to be right again, Shane. Great work!"

"Thanks. I'm going to take those days off now and go to Paisley," Shane said.

"Good luck and if you need anything, please call," Jason said.

At one point during his time at the OPP Detachment in Simcoe, Shane had called Emma to very briefly explain what was going on and tell her he didn't know what time he would be home. Emma said she was anxious to hear all of the details but thought they should wait until after Lan had gone to bed, and Shane agreed.

This morning, before he left for Paisley, he had breakfast with Emma and Lan, and he was pleased to see that the young girl seemed to be in good spirits, chatting about how she could hardly wait to be allowed to go to school and refusing any help with her cereal and toast, saying with a smile that she was doing just fine learning to use her left hand. Shane thought the fact that Lan didn't wake up screaming in the middle of the night because of a nightmare related to the death of her parents was a good sign that she was starting to heal psychologically from the trauma she had suffered.

After breakfast, Lan went to the living room to watch television and Shane put his overnight bag near the front door.

"Are you still sure you're okay with me going?" Shane asked. "If you have any concerns at all about Lan's safety, I'll stay until they arrest the members of the gang."

"I think it's important that you go and get some answers," Emma said and then put her arms around Shane and kissed him. "You know that I can look after myself and you've made sure the house is secure."

Shane did know that Emma was more than capable of defending herself and Lan. She'd received extensive hand-to-hand combat and weapons training when she was a member of the Canadian Forces, she kept herself in excellent shape and joined Shane regularly at the gun range.

"I realize you have a tough time remembering codes, but you're okay with the lock box in the bedroom?" Shane asked. He kept a Glock 19 pistol in a small gun safe at the bottom of one of the nightstands.

"032047, my Dad's birthday," Emma answered.

"And you'll have to memorize the codes for the updated home security system so they're not on that sticky note you currently have on the fridge door," Shane said.

"Yes, boss," Emma said, kissed Shane again and then asked, "You sure you don't want to take my Jeep to Paisley and leave your black death trap at home?"

"No, I'm fine with the Charger," Shane said and then added, "And for the thousandth time, it's not a death trap, it's a classic."

"Okay, it's a classic death trap," Emma deadpanned.

Chapter Eighteen

As Shane drove slowly along Paisley's main street, he thought about how circumstances kept drawing him back to the hometown he had such a love-hate relationship with.

The village had a population of approximately a thousand residents and was located in rural southwestern Ontario at the junction of the Teeswater and Saugeen rivers, the latter being very popular for canoeing and fishing. The downtown area had the usual kind of businesses, such as a grocery store and hardware, but it also featured several unique gift shops which attracted a large number of tourists every year.

Shane had a great childhood growing up in Paisley; he and his friend Ben Chen spent countless hours fishing and swimming in the Saugeen in the summer and tobogganing on the hills in the area during the winter.

Shane's father, Ed Daniels, had an auto repair shop in an old gas station on the southern edge of the village, and Shane enjoyed helping out after school and during summers. However, like many young people who grew up in a small town, Shane dreamed about getting away from Paisley as soon as he could. His father believed Shane had the talent to become one of the few Canadians playing in the NBA, but he didn't want to pursue a professional basketball career, he was determined to become a cop, which he did. But his dream career was cut short when he was shot responding to a domestic dispute.

Shane's relationship with Paisley started to sour when he was seventeen years old and solved the murder of Alina Ivanov, the young, married Russian immigrant he was having an affair with. And he vowed never to come back after he had his father arrested for murder. However, after he met Emma, she convinced him to return to Paisley as a way of exorcising some of his demons, particularly his feelings towards his father. Emma fell in love with Paisley and so they began visiting there regularly on their way to the Lake Huron tourist town of Port Elgin to camp at the nearby McGregor Provincial Park.

The last time Shane was drawn back to Paisley was when his childhood friend, Ben, was arrested for murdering his elderly neighbour, but he managed to prove that Ben was innocent.

On his way out of Paisley, Shane pulled into the gas station where he often filled up the Charger on his way to Port Elgin, but he had another reason for stopping today. He was hoping that Doug Connelly, the elderly, retired man who worked part-time at the station would be there so he could arrange a meeting to talk to him. Doug was retired from the Bruce Nuclear Generating Station located on the shore of Lake Huron and would have a very comfortable pension, but he had told Shane during one of Shane's earlier stops that he got bored sitting at home, didn't like to golf and didn't have any hobbies, so he worked at the gas station for something to do. Shane suspected Doug enjoyed talking to the locals while he filled up their vehicles so he could keep up on the local gossip and that was why Shane wanted to talk to him; he would be an excellent source of information about what was being said around Paisley about the murders.

Shane stopped the Charger at the gas pumps, got out of the car, and was pleased to see Connelly coming out of the attendant's kiosk. Doug was a tall man, almost as tall as Shane, thin, with a very erect posture, gray hair cut very close to his scalp, and dark-rimmed glasses.

"Well, if it isn't Shane Daniels back in town," Connelly said as he approached the Charger.

"Hello, Mr. Connelly, how're you doing?" Shane asked pleasantly.

"Not bad for an old fella and it's Doug. Mr. Connelly makes me sound older than I already am," Connelly replied.

Shane told the elderly man to fill up the car and once he had the pump going, he asked Shane, "Do I assume you're here because of the bodies of that woman and child they found in the woods?"

"I am, as a matter of fact," Shane answered.

"It's a terrible tragedy, the worst thing that's happened around here in a long, long time," Connelly said sincerely and then added, "The cops are getting nowhere with it, but maybe now that Paisley's famous Detective is here, we can find out who did it."

Shane's name was well known in the area because he had solved his mother's murder, cleared Ben Chen of a murder charge and there had been media coverage of other cases he had been involved with.

"I don't know about famous, but I am planning to investigate the murders," Shane said.

After Doug finished filling up the Charger and processing Shane's credit card, Shane asked, "Do you still belong to the Legion, Doug?"

"I've been known to have an ale or two there," Doug said with a smile.

"I was wondering whether, after you're finished work later today, if you would sign me in as a guest so I can buy you a beer and you can bring me up to date on what's been happening around town?" Shane asked.

Doug's eyes lit up and he said, "I'd be more than happy to do that."

Shane knew that Doug Connelly wouldn't resist the opportunity to sit in the Legion with him and look important to his buddies, plus share any local gossip he had about the murders. Shane was counting on that.

After leaving the gas station, Shane drove to Port Elgin to meet with his friend Ben Chen at the Chinese buffet restaurant Ben owned. Just as he had during his drive between Brantford and Simcoe, he took in the display of colourful leaves on the Maple trees along the way. The summer tourist season was over so there wasn't the usual congestion along the town's main thoroughfare and the parking lot of Ben's restaurant actually had some spots available.

Shane entered the restaurant and was greeted by the Hostess who recognized him and said Ben was at his usual spot, so he entered the main dining area and turned to the first table on the right where Ben normally sat.

When Ben saw him walking up to the table, he got a big smile on his face, stood up, and said. "Look at what the fucking cat dragged in! Shit, I guess I shouldn't say cat out loud in a Chinese restaurant!"

Ben, as usual, laughed out loud at his own tasteless joke and looked around at the people sitting at nearby tables to see if he got a reaction which, if he did, would amuse him to no end.

After a brief hug, Shane and Ben sat at the table and Ben asked, "How the fuck are you?"

"I'm not bad, Ben, getting by," Shane answered.

Shane and Ben had been close and loyal friends since they were kids growing up together in Paisley even though they were complete opposites, both physically and in personality. Shane was tall and Ben was quite short, Shane had a workout regime that kept him in good shape while Ben claimed he was allergic to exercise. Ben had been big for most of his life, but he had lost a lot of weight in recent years, most of it while he was in jail awaiting trial for a murder that Shane proved he didn't commit.

While Shane's blue eyes and heavy beard compared to Ben's light complexion and Asian features made them physical opposites, that was nothing compared to their personalities. Shane was a thinker and most often soft-spoken while Ben was loud and brash, and couldn't seem to finish a sentence with some type of swear word in it. The swearing always bothered Emma, especially if the three of them were out in public, but she liked Ben and tolerated his language because she knew how close he and Shane were. Shane considered his friend to be the most socially and politically incorrect person he had ever met and had told Ben that many times over the years, but secretly always got a real kick out of Ben's antics.

Ben's Chinese buffet restaurant, which he inherited from his parents, was very successful, but that was not the primary reason he was a very wealthy man. Ben was a talented video game designer and his work was always in demand by the big name game studios. Despite his wealth, Ben lived modestly, including living in his parent's home in Paisley after they both passed away.

"So, fill me in on everything that's going on," Ben said as he pulled his chair up closer to the table and clasped his hands in front of him.

Shane first told him about his just completed Matheson case and the couple's willingness to live apart for seven years, her under a false identity, to collect one and a quarter million dollars in life insurance.

"Clever motherfuckers," Ben commented. "One and a quarter million won't seem like a lot of money to some people for what the Mathesons did, but probably to them it was worth the seven years to get what they thought would put them on fucking easy street for the rest of their lives."

Although Shane had earlier given Ben an outline on the phone about the discovery that he had a half-sister, he now provided his friend with the details.

"I'm so fucking sorry you learned you had a sister but will never get to know her," Ben said sincerely. "And I know it makes it worse that her and her mother's bodies were found in the same woods where your mother and Alina were buried."

"I've been trying not to think about that," Shane responded. "But I do have to consider the possibility they're connected somehow and not just a coincidence."

"So, what's your plan, and what do you need me to do?" Ben asked.

"I was hoping I could stay at your place while I was in Paisley," Shane said.

"Fuck off for even asking!" Ben exclaimed.

"Thanks," Shane responded and then said, "I know the police have been interviewing people in town in an effort to identify the woman and her daughter, but a lot of them may be reluctant to tell the cops anything because they don't want to get involved. I was hoping you'd spend some time in town with me talking to people you know, see what we can come up with."

"You can fucking count on me," Ben said and then asked about the situation with Emma and the young girl, saying he was surprised that, as he put it, "Emma had gone all domestic".

"Lan is a special young girl who has gone through a lot and there's no question that Emma has fallen in love with her," Shane said. "And I am worried about what impact it's going to have on Emma when the time comes for Lan to go to a permanent foster home."

"I'm sure it will be fine, Emma's a fucking rock," Ben said.

"I'm not so sure," Shane said softly and after a moment's hesitation while he thought about it, he brightened up and asked Ben, "What about you? What have you been up to?"

"I met someone," Ben said.

"Really! Good for you Ben! Finally!" Shane said excitedly. "Tell me about her. It is a her, right?"

"Of course, it's a fucking her," Ben said irritably.

"Ben, I seem to remember you telling me that you thought you might be gay," Shane said.

He was just giving Ben a hard time, turning the tables on a guy who took great joy in saying things to shock people or get under their skin. Ben's idea that he might be gay, which he told Shane during a recent telephone conversation, fell into that category.

"Oh, well, about that," Ben said sheepishly. "I thought it over and I decided it wasn't going to work for me. I realized the only man I was attracted to was you, you tall, handsome fucker!"

"I can see that," Shane deadpanned.

The two friends looked at each other for a moment and then started laughing, did a fist bump and Ben slapped the table for emphasis, drawing the attention of some of the customers sitting around them.

After they calmed down, Shawn repeated, "So, tell me about her."

"Her name's Michelle Watson," Ben said. "She's an artist who lives in Toronto but has a winterized cottage just outside of town that she uses as a year-round studio. She works primarily in watercolours doing landscapes from around the area and you wouldn't believe how fucking beautiful they are."

"How'd you meet?" Shane asked.

"She came into the restaurant one night and I just happened to be standing near the entrance," Ben answered. "She whispered to me, 'Is the food any good here?' and I said, 'What, because I'm Chinese I'm supposed to automatically be a fucking expert on Chinese food?'"

"That sounds like something you would say," Shane commented.

"And you know what she said when I asked her that?" Ben continued, "She smiled at me and said, 'Of course', and didn't blink an eye. I liked her right away."

"That's a real love story," Shane said sarcastically.

"I want you to meet her," Ben said. "I texted her to let her know you were here and she's coming over."

Shane and Ben talked about a strategy to try and get any information they could from around Paisley about the bodies found in the woods. Shane said he was meeting with Doug Connelly at the Legion later in the day for a beer and Ben thought that was a great idea, saying Doug always asked him a lot of personal questions whenever he was at the station to get gas and probably did the same with everyone.

After about fifteen minutes, Ben looked out the window beside their table and said, "Here she is."

Shane watched as a powerful looking Suzuki motorcycle, the type often called a 'crotch rocket', pulled into a parking spot. Its rider, dressed in tight black leather motorcycle pants and a matching waist length jacket, dismounted the bike and took off her helmet, which allowed her long raven-coloured hair to spill onto her shoulders.

Michelle was medium height, making her taller than Ben, and very thin. Her dark hair was parted in the middle, framing a pale face with a petite nose, pencilled eyebrows, thickly applied dark eyeliner and thin lips painted a bright red. Michelle's nose featured three tiny rings on the left nostril and each earlobe was lined with multiple rings.

Shane thought to himself that while Michelle was not his type, he knew that a lot of men would find her very attractive.

Michelle left her helmet on the seat of the bike, walked into the restaurant, and when she reached their table, Shane and Ben stood up. She gave Ben a quick kiss and Shane watched his friend's face light up like a kid on Christmas morning. Michelle then stuck out her hand at Shane and said in a noticeably raspy voice, "I'm Michelle Watson and you must be the Shane Daniels I've heard so much about from Ben, who says you're a brilliant private detective."

"Brilliant private detective is a little over the top," Shane responded. "I work as an investigator for a law firm and most of what I do is pretty boring."

They all sat down and Shane noticed that the normally brash Ben looked nervous and hesitant when he said to Michelle, "I told Shane about you being an artist and how good your watercolours are."

"Thanks. Some of my work has turned out not too bad, but the rest is totally fucking shit, not even decent enough to be considered works in progress," Michelle said.

"You're too fucking hard on yourself," Ben said as he put his hand over Michelle's.

Michelle leaned close to Ben and said, "It doesn't matter if I'm hard on myself, Benny, as long as your fucking hard when you're around me."

Benny? Did she just call Ben, 'Benny', and he let her do it? Shane asked himself. He must really like this Michelle. They most certainly have the foul language thing in common, Shane thought.

Chapter Nineteen

An hour and a half later, after he, Ben and Michelle drank coffee and discussed a number of topics, Shane parked along the main street in Paisley and walked to the Legion to meet Doug Connelly for a beer.

Shane wasn't sure yet what to make of Michelle. She was quite talkative and with Ben being the same way, he was surprised they didn't clash in that regard, but Ben let her lead the conversation, content to just sit at the table with a grin on his face. Shane thought it was obvious that Ben had fallen hard for Michelle and if that was the case, he would fully support his friend.

The Paisley Legion was located in the historic town hall building near the cenotaph and was one of the village's unique landmarks. Doug was waiting for Shane at the front door and together they went up the interior stairs to the large room that had been converted into the Legion's main lounge. Shane bought them beers, they sat down at a small table near a corner, and he looked around at the large crowd of people enjoying late day drinks.

"Busy place," Shane commented.

"It's one of the few places around here where you can go and drink, and play either cards, shuffleboard or darts," Doug said and then took a healthy swig of beer. "When I was a younger man, we all used to go to the Paisley Inn to drink and listen to music. You remember that building?"

"I do," Shane said. The Inn, a three-storey orange brick building, had been located in the center of the village, but after years of being closed and falling into disrepair, it was torn down.

"So, Doug, the reason I wanted to get together with you is because not only are you a life-long resident of Paisley, but you work at a busy gas station and come in contact with a lot of local people over the course of a week," Shane said.

"That I do," Doug said and Shane noticed that Doug had already finished his beer before Shane had even taken his first drink, so he got up, went to the bar and bought two more, figuring Doug could have his if he was going to drink that fast.

After he returned to the table and Doug started working on his second beer, Shane said, "The place where they found the bodies is remote, well away from any highway, which means it wasn't chosen randomly. The killer knew the area, and, to me, that confirms he's local."

Shane knew it was also confirmed by the fact his dad was the father of the child, but he had no intention of telling anyone that.

"Someone in Paisley knows something," Shane continued, "Have you heard any gossip or rumours, anything at all?"

"Well, as you can imagine, it's been a big topic of conversation," Doug said. "Everyone, except for tourists passing through, mentions it when they come into the station for gas or to buy snacks. Lots of people are worried there's a killer on the loose and say they're locking their doors at night, and there are complaints the police aren't doing enough to find out who's responsible. But I can't say that anyone's said anything to me that made me think they might know something useful."

"What about the woman and her child?" Shane asked. "Has anyone suggested or speculated who they might be?"

"Everyone I've talked to is convinced they're not from around here," Doug replied. "It's a small town and as soon as those bodies were found, someone would have thought of someone they knew and they hadn't seen around recently. A few names got tossed around and some were even given to the police, but they were all found safe and sound, and had only been out of sight because either they were sick or away on vacation."

"Well, as I said, someone must know something. I just have to find them," Shane said.

By this time Doug had consumed his second beer and after he set the empty bottle on the table, he put his fist to his mouth to stifle a burp and then said, "We should be talking to Biggie, I'm sure he hears lots of stuff. I'll go get us another beer, get him to take a break and come and sit with us."

Doug got up from the table and after Shane put up his hand and said he didn't need another beer and would work on the two he already had, the elderly man, who seemed to have an empty leg when it came to beer, headed for the bar.

Biggie, whose real name was Johann Gertson, was the Legion's long-time bartender and Shane wondered why he wasn't long retired because he had to have been at least in his late seventies. Biggie got his nickname because he was big; a mountain of a man with wide arms and tree-trunk legs, thick fat hands, a huge bald head sitting on a wide, fleshy neck and a crooked boxer's nose.

Nobody dared cause any trouble in the Legion when Biggie was behind the bar. When Shane was young, he and Ben were always speculating about the German-Canadian's background and because they found him to be gruff and humourless, they were convinced he'd been a member of the Nazi SS during the war. Quite frankly, they were afraid of the man and it didn't help that he sounded like the Nazis speaking English in the old war movies they watched.

"You vill move out of za vay!" He remembered Gertson barking at him when Shane worked at the grocery store and was blocking a shelf Gertson wanted to get to.

Shane watched as Doug went to the bar, got another beer, and started talking to Biggie, at one point gesturing in Shane's direction and the bartender looked over at him. After about ten minutes, Doug returned to the table with Biggie, who was wiping his hands on his white apron, and they both sat down.

"Biggie, you remember Shane Daniels? His dad ran the repair shop?" Doug asked.

"Ya, his dad killed somebody and vent to prison," Biggie said in a flat, matter of fact way and looked at Shane with no expression on his face. Shane noticed that Gertson hadn't lost much of his heavy German accent over the years and still didn't even have a hint of friendliness on his face.

"Did Doug explain what I'm doing in town and what I'm looking for?" Shane asked Gertson.

"I did," Doug said before Gertson could answer. "And he says he just thought of something but isn't sure if it's relevant."

"Do you mind telling me anyway, Mr. Gertson? I'm looking for anything," Shane said to Biggie.

Gertson crossed his big arms, which Shane saw had gone flabby with age, and didn't say anything for a moment, just continued to stare at him. He's an old man, but I still find him frightening, Shane thought.

Gertson finally spoke and said there are two men, both in their late twenties, who come into the Legion on a regular basis, mostly Saturdays, and drink for several hours. They aren't locals, Gertson said, and they speak with what he called a Newfie accent, which Shane took to mean they were from one of the eastern provinces. Gertson figured they worked on one of the big dairy or beef farms in the area because a lot of men from the east came to Ontario looking for work. He said that one Saturday when the two men were in the Legion, after they had a lot to drink, he overheard them arguing about a young woman. One of the men had said something about not believing she was related to the old man and wondered why she never left the farm. He also said that she was hot and he'd really like to screw her. The other guy got angry and told him to shut up about the woman and that he knew he was supposed to stay away from her and, besides, the boss told him she was pregnant.

"When was this?" Shane asked.

"I don't know, couple of years ago," Gertson said and then added, "But I remembered overhearing that argument because the two guys came in for a beer recently and I thought it was unusual to see them on a weekday. They had another heated discussion, I was too busy to hear what it was about, but at one point I did hear one of them saying loudly, 'I'm telling you it's her and we can cash in'. They left after only having one drink. Seeing them having that discussion reminded me of the argument they had a couple of years ago."

"Do you know their names?" Shane asked.

"I'm not one hundred percent sure, but I think the one who did most of the talking was Jack," Gertson said. "I think the other one's name started with an M, maybe Melvin or something like that."

"And you're sure their farmhands?" Shane asked. He knew that a lot of men came from the east to work at the Bruce Generating Station.

"What, you don't think I know what a farm worker looks like!?" Gertson said gruffly.

It came out as, "Vawt, you don zinc I know what zee farm worker lookz like!?" and Shane wondered how, after living his entire adult life in Paisley and working for decades at the Legion, Gertson had managed to hang on to his thick German accent.

Shane then asked, "Have you told the cops about any of this?"

Gertson just stared at him again and got a look on his face like he thought Shane was stupid.

"Didn't I say I just remembered it?" Gertson snapped.

"Sorry, yes you did," Shane responded sheepishly and then asked, "Can you give me a description of these two guys?"

Gertson told Shane what he remembered about the men and Shane made notes in the thin reporter's notebook he always carried with him. When the bartender finished giving Shane what he could in regards to descriptions of the two men, Shane said, "Thanks for telling me about this, Mr. Gertson."

Gertson didn't say anything, he just got up from the table and walked back to the bar. He hasn't changed much, he's still a big friendly guy, Shane thought, smiling to himself.

"This could be something, don't you think?" Doug said as he pushed aside his latest empty beer, reached across the table and grabbed one of the full ones sitting in from of Shane. Boy, this old guy can really put it away, Shane thought.

"Yes, it's definitely worth checking out. I need to see if I can find those farm workers," Shane said and then added, "You've been a great help, Doug. I'm going to give you my card with my cell number on it and if you think of anything else, give me a call."

"I most certainly will and I'll ask around about those farmhands. Somebody here at the Legion should know something about them," Doug said.

Shane stood up to leave and asked, "Would you like a ride home?" He was worried that after all of the beer Doug had consumed in a short period of time that he would drive home.

"No, I going to stay here for a bit and talk to some of the folks. I might get some info for you. Then I'm going to walk home," Doug said.

I sure hope he can still walk by then, Shane thought.

After leaving the Legion, Shane walked to one of the nearby restaurants and had something to eat. After he was finished, he went to where he parked the Charger and drove to Ben's house, which was located on a quiet street not far from a public park and the Saugeen River.

After he was accused, and then cleared of the murder of his elderly next door neighbour, Shane thought Ben would sell his house and move, either elsewhere in Paisley or to Port Elgin where he would be closer to his restaurant. But because it was his parent's house, Ben felt an attachment to it and said he had no plans to sell.

When Shane got to the house and parked out front, he knew that Ben was home because his huge, fire engine red, F150 Ford pickup was in the driveway. Shane could never figure out why Ben wanted a big pickup, especially one that short in stature Ben had to literally climb up into. According to Ben, he owned the F150 so he could drive around and smile at the local rednecks who he claimed wouldn't be happy about seeing a Chinese guy driving a big pickup like theirs.

When Shane walked into the house, Ben had just finished eating and was cleaning up the kitchen. While he did that, Shane took his overnight bag into the guest bedroom and then called Emma. She said that she and Lan were waiting for a pizza to arrive and after they ate and Lan had a bath, they were going to watch a movie.

"She's such a sweetheart, so smart and gifted, we're having a great time together," Emma gushed on the phone.

Am I talking to the same tough, independent woman I live with? Shane asked himself. This young girl has unlocked a completely different side of Emma and Shane wasn't sure what to make of it.

Shane told Emma about his visit to the Legion and his conversation with the bartender and Emma agreed it was a promising lead. Shane reminded Emma to call him if looking after Lan became too much, but she assured him everything was fine.

After finishing his call with Emma, Shane and Ben sat at the kitchen table and Shane gave him a detailed recounting of what Mr. Gertson told him at the Legion.

"I don't go into the Legion," Ben said and then asked, "Is Gertson still a fucking big, bald, friendly, cuddly bear?"

"Pretty much," Shane said and they both laughed. "He's quite old now but he still, quite frankly, scares the shit out of me."

"That's the reason why I don't into the Legion," Ben said. "Gertson would remember me from when I was a kid and I don't think I could handle his fucking death stare."

"We need to find those two farm hands," Shane said, changing the subject back to what he learned today. There's a good possibility the young woman they were talking about is the woman found buried in the woods."

"Or she could be a woman who's alive and well, and known around town," Ben said.

"Could be, but I keep thinking about Gertson overhearing them say they didn't believe the woman was a relative of the owner and that she never left the farm," Shane said. "That would mean she wasn't known in town and if she went missing, no one would know."

"How about this," Ben said. "Tomorrow we do a canvass of the local stores and ask about farm workers who come in on a regular basis who fit the descriptions that Gertson gave you."

"That's what I was thinking," Shane said. "Hopefully, we can get some names or better yet, where they work."

"Okay, we're good to fucking go!" Ben said enthusiastically, but Shane could see by the expression on Ben's face that he had something else on his mind.

Shane had purposely not mentioned anything about Ben's new girlfriend because he knew not saying anything would drive his friend crazy. They'd been playing these kinds of mind games on each other since they were kids and Ben took great delight in doing it to Shane, so he was happy he was able to take a turn.

"Was there something you wanted to ask me, Ben?" Shane said, trying to keep a straight face.

"You're an asshole, Daniels, you know that, right?" Ben said. "You haven't said one word about Michelle since you got to the house."

"Oh, you mean the biker bunny in leather I met today?" Shane asked seriously.

"You're a real fucking comedian, you should go on the road," Ben said.

"I liked her, Ben," Shane said. "She came across as very intelligent."

"Yea, she's super fucking smart," Ben said. "Besides her excellent artwork, she does some writing and knows a lot about gaming, has even tried her hand at programming."

"That alone will give you a lot in common," Shane remarked.

"We're thinking about doing a project together. She's got a couple of ideas I think have promise," Ben said.

Ben had been through a lot over the past couple of years, not the least of which was being in jail accused of murder, plus the deaths of both his parents, so Shane was pleased to see his friend's face light up when he talked about Michelle.

"As I told you at the restaurant today, I'm really happy for you Ben and I hope things work out with Michelle," Shane said.

"Me too. I was getting tired of having to spend time with girls you had to blow up," Ben deadpanned.

"Now who should go on the road?" Shane responded.

Chapter Twenty

Emma sat at her kitchen table working on her laptop, catching up on emails, paying some bills, checking her monthly budget and moving a few investments around to secure a higher yield.

Lan was in her room with headphones on and watching videos on the tablet Shane had bought for her and while Emma knew she shouldn't be concerned, she couldn't help herself from worrying about whether the internet parental controls were working properly on the tablet. They were all set up when Shane gave Lan the tablet so it should be okay, Emma thought, but maybe I'll double-check after Lan has gone to bed.

Oh my God, I'm starting to turn into my mother! Emma told herself, remembering how her mom worried about everything Emma did. When she was in her rebellious teenage years and she and her mom would get into arguments about it, Emma used to accuse her of being paranoid. Now she knows what it was like for her mom.

All of that aside, Emma's greater worry was about Lan's mental well-being. While the nightmares that had Lan waking up screaming at night appeared to have come to an end and she seemed to be happy most of the time, Emma knew she was still struggling with what had happened to her. She was putting on a brave face, but there had been several occasions when she didn't think Emma was watching that Lan's lips would tremble and tears would run down her face as she stared at the stump on her right arm. Emma had already spent a lot of time talking to Lan about how things would be better once she had her prosthetic and she believed Lan would get a lot of help during her sessions with Emma's friend, Psychiatrist Charlene Anderson.

Emma had been quite upset earlier in the evening because of a visit by Maggie Sawyer from FACS and the news she had. Maggie said that the police have, so far, been unable to track down the two members of the Vietnamese gang that Lan identified as the men who ran the marijuana extraction lab in the basement of her house and were responsible for running her parent's vehicle off the highway.

"It's possible they're staying out of sight in a house or apartment owned by another member of the gang," Maggie said. "Or they've fled the province, maybe even the country."

"If they've fled the country back to Vietnam, that would be the best case scenario," Emma said.

But as worrisome as it was that the two men were still at large, that was not the news Maggie had that upset Emma.

"I wanted you to know that I have found a Vietnamese couple here in the city that are willing to take Lan in, first as foster parents, but would be willing, depending on how things go, to adopt her," Maggie said.

"Oh, well, that's good news," Emma said flatly. She couldn't bring herself to try and act happy.

Maggie picked up on this and said, "Emma, I know that you've come to care a lot about Lan, but we felt it would be in her best interest to be around people from her own culture, to allow her to grow up retaining her native language and traditions. And don't forget you're going to continue to see Lan a lot, helping her adjust after her stump has fully healed and she has been fitted with a prosthetic arm."

"What about Lan's safety until those two men are caught?" Emma asked. "No one knows she's here and we have great security. More importantly, Lan feels safe here."

"I'm aware of that and that's why nothing's going to happen right away," Maggie responded.

"And what about Lan? Will she get a say on where she lives?" Emma asked, trying not to sound desperate.

"Emma, you knew that Lan staying with you was only short term," Maggie answered.

After Maggie left, Emma felt a wave of depression descend upon her and it took all of her willpower not to cry. Maggie's news about the Vietnamese family was the right decision for Lan, Emma knew that, but she also knew that Lan leaving would break her heart.

Emma looked at the time on the kitchen clock, and realized it was getting late and that it was past time for Lan to be in bed. She closed the laptop, went to Lan's room where the door was partially open, knocked gently, and entered. Because Lan was wearing headphones and was completely focused on the tablet, Emma had to touch her on the shoulder to get her attention.

Lan looked up, took off the headphones, smiled, and said, "Hi Emma!" Emma couldn't help it, she felt herself getting emotional and took Lan in her arms and hugged her tight.

Ever since Lan moved in, Emma had become a light sleeper, worried that Lan would have a nightmare and she wouldn't hear her call out. That night, long after Lan had gone to sleep, Emma suddenly came wide awake and it was not because of Lan. She heard a noise she was very familiar with; when it was quiet, you could always hear the floor in the front hallway creaking when someone walked on it. When her parents were still alive and Emma lived at home, she used to try and sneak into the house and down the hall to her bedroom, but the noisy floor betrayed her every time and the next morning her parents would drill her about where she was until so late.

Emma listened intently and heard it again, the floor creaking in the hall. The bathroom was right next to Lan's bedroom, so it wasn't her. That meant that someone was in the house! Why didn't the alarm go off? The system had both a silent remote signal to a security company and a loud piercing alarm that went off in the house. Didn't I set the alarm before I went to bed? Emma asked herself in a panic, but she was positive that she did.

Emma threw back the bed covers, reached over the side of the bed, grabbed her prosthetic leg off the floor, sat up, and quickly put it on.

She always wore just a t-shirt and boxer shorts to bed but didn't bother putting on a robe out of fear it would restrict her movement.

Emma got down on one knee and opened the door on the bottom of the nightstand to get at the small gun safe. What's the combination!? The panic had made Emma's mind go blank. Think! Seconds felt like minutes as Emma calmed herself down. My father's birth date, that's it!

Emma opened the safe, picked up the Glock pistol, inserted the magazine, and silently pulled back the slide on the top of the gun to load a round.

Getting quickly to her feet, Emma went to the bedroom door and took a quick look around the frame, down the hallway to her right toward the front door. There was some light because of the nightlights Emma had plugged into two receptacles at the base of the hallway wall for Lan in case she got up during the night, and from a small fluorescent light over the sink in the kitchen which she always left on.

In the dim light, Emma could see a man walking down the hallway toward her. He was young, short, dressed in dark jeans and a jean jacket, and had Asian features.

Emma stepped into the hallway holding the pistol in the standard two-handed grip, pointed the gun at the man and yelled, "Put your hands up over your head, get down on your knees and then lay face down on the floor! Do it now or I will shoot you!"

The man put his hands up but didn't move to get down.

"Get down on the floor!" Emma called out and then added, "Xuong!" because she wasn't sure if the man spoke English. Lan had been teaching her some basic words in Vietnamese like hello, goodbye, thank you, in and out, and up and down. If Emma remembered correctly, she had shouted at the intruder to get down. This time, he quickly spread out face down on the floor.

Suddenly, Emma heard Lan scream in terror, but it sounded muffled. Keeping the gun aimed at the man on the floor, Emma started backing up quickly toward Lan's bedroom. She felt movement behind her, turned slightly, and looked over her right shoulder just in time to see another man, with a knife in his hand, advancing on her.

Emma spun and managed to hit her attacker on the head with the gun in her hands, but his forward momentum kept him going and he slammed into Emma, sending her down to the floor on her back. Somehow she managed to hold on to the gun.

The man, who had fallen to the floor at the end of Emma's feet, raised his arm holding the knife over his head and plunged it down on her leg, but it was her prosthetic made of titanium so all the tip of the blade hit was metal.

On her back, Emma aimed down and fired the gun into her assailant's forehead resulting in a small entry wound at the front and a spray of blood, bone and brain out the back of his head.

Expecting that the other intruder had gotten off the floor and was going to attack, Emma rolled onto her stomach and pointed the gun in front of her. But instead of coming toward Emma, the man had turned and was quickly making his way to the front door. Emma aimed and shot him through the back of his right knee, sending him to the floor howling in pain.

Emma knew the guy wouldn't be going anywhere, but while he moaned and rolled back and forth holding his destroyed knee with both hands to try and stem the bleeding, she checked him over for weapons and found a hunting knife in a sheath on his belt. She removed the knife and took it with her as she quickly made her way to Lan's room. Once inside, she turned on the overhead light, put her gun and knife on top of a nearby dresser, and went to Lan's bed, but she wasn't there!

Panic gripped Emma. What did that guy do with Lan!? She started toward the closet to check inside, but first dropped onto her knees and looked under the bed where she saw Lan huddling and gripping one of her stuffies with both hands.

"Lan, sweetheart, are you okay?" Emma said as she reached out and put her hand on the side of Lan's face.

"I heard someone walking in the house and I just knew it wasn't you, Emma," Lan said softly, her voice trembling. "I hid under the bed and tried to be quiet, but a man found me and I screamed."

"You were very brave," Emma said, fighting back tears. "You can come out now, everything's okay."

Lan crawled out from under the bed and Emma sat on the floor and held her tightly in her arms. She could hear the man she shot in the knee moaning from the pain and speaking loudly in Vietnamese. She suspected it was mostly cursing.

"Someone is still here?" Lan asked nervously.

"Yes, but he's badly hurt, so you don't have to worry about him," Emma said and then added, "Lan, I'm going to get up and call the police, and I need you to stay here in your room, no matter what. I need to go keep an eye on the man you can hear, but I'll always be close by and I'll come and check on you a lot. Can you do that for me?"

"I'll be okay, Emma," Lan said and this time Emma couldn't stop her tears.

Chapter Twenty One

It was over a week before Shane was able to return to Paisley and follow up on the lead he had on the possible identities of the young woman and her daughter, his half-sister, whose bodies were found in the woods. And even then, he was very reluctant to leave Emma and Lan.

The night Emma shot the two men, she called the police and then immediately called Shane at Ben's house and gave him a quick explanation of what happened. Although he had been in a deep sleep, Shane was out of bed and immediately alert, asking Emma if she and Lan had been hurt. Emma told him Lan was fine and she wasn't injured, just a bit shaky as the shock of what happened started to set in. Shane said he was on his way and told her that when the police arrived, she wasn't to give them anything more than the basic details of what happened until he got there. Shane didn't want the police to ask Emma a lot of questions while she was still in shock and trying to process what happened.

After he hung up from talking to Emma, Shane grabbed a quick shower, made coffee to put in a thermos that he found in a kitchen cupboard, and then woke Ben to tell him what was going on. Ben wanted to go with him to help out, but Shane told him to stay behind and keep working on the case.

Shane broke the speed limit during the entire drive home and using all of the shortcuts and back roads he knew, he was back in Brantford in just over two hours.

When he arrived at the house, there were still two cruisers parked in front of the house, along with a white forensics van and a dark police SUV. Police tape had been strung from the left post on the front step, down above the front lawn, around the maple trees on both sides of the end of the walkway and then back up to the post on the other side of the front door. A police Constable was standing inside the tape on the sidewalk to keep the curious onlookers, and there were five or six of them, away from the house and on the other side of the street. Shane told the officer who he was and when asked, showed identification before being allowed in his house.

Shane stopped to look at the front door and saw that some type of instrument was used to disable both the regular lock and the deadbolt. The two men were obviously well trained on how to gain silent entry into locked buildings.

Once inside the house, Shane saw two forensic specialists, both wearing white Tyvek coveralls, working in the hallway between the kitchen and the bedrooms. One of them, a woman, was on her knees using a Q-tip to collect a sample from a large dark stain of presumably blood on the hardwood floor.

Shane looked to his right into the living room and saw Emma and Lan sitting close together on the couch. Emma was wearing a dark blue tracksuit and Shane could see the dark circles under her eyes from lack of sleep. Lan was in a pink housecoat over her pyjamas, white fluffy slippers and holding one of the many stuffies that Emma had bought for her. Across from them, on chairs they had brought in from the kitchen, were Sgt. Wyatt Lincoln of the Brant Police Service and Sgt. Gurdeep Singh of the RCMP, both of whom Shane knew were working on Lan's case. When they saw him, both Emma and Lan rushed over and hugged Shane, who was surprised, but pleased, that Lan had joined in.

"Are you both okay?" Shane said as the three of them held onto each other. "I can't believe this happened, I've been really worried."

In response, Emma whispered firmly in Shane's ear, "I'm fine. I was in shock for a while after it happened, but now I'm not having any problems. I did what I had to do to protect Lan and myself, and I would do it again."

Shane then knelt in front of Lan and asked, "And what about you Lan? How are you? You've been through a really scary experience."

Even though Emma whispered, Lan must have heard what she said to Shane because she responded to his question with, "I'm okay, just like Emma. She protected me."

"Yes, she did. I'm very proud of her," Shane said and gave Lan another hug.

"I'm sorry to interrupt, but there are some things I would like to discuss," Sgt. Singh said as he stood up from his chair.

"In a minute, Sergeant, but first I would like to have a word with Emma in private," Shane responded and then said to Lan, "Can you stay here with the two police officers while I talk to Emma?"

"I'll go sit on the couch and wait for you," Lan replied.

Shane and Emma walked into the kitchen and before he said anything, Shane gave her a long kiss. When they parted, he said, "What the hell happened!? How did they get into the house without setting off the silent alarm at the security company and the siren in here? They can't cut the power because the system runs on a battery. Did you somehow forget to set it last night?"

"Shane, you have to believe me when I say that I'm one hundred percent positive that I set the alarm before I went to bed," Emma said in a firm voice. "I distinctly remember setting the system and then checking to make sure the deadbolts were in place at both the front and back doors."

"After the shooting, did anyone check to see if the system was on or off?" Shane asked.

"I did and it was off, but I know I turned it on last night," Emma said, the frustration evident in her voice. "They must have had the code, it's the only explanation."

"If that's the case, we need to find out how they got it," Shane said.

"Could someone have hacked into the security company's server to get the code?" Emma asked.

"It's possible, but unlikely," Shane answered. "Logan Security is the best in the city, that's why I use them, and I know that all of their data is encrypted, but I will check with them just in case."

"Maybe someone working at Logan sold our entry code to the Vietnamese gang," Emma suggested.

"It's another possibility I'll have to check out," Shane said.

The idea that someone sold the entry code to the intruders had Emma thinking about something that she didn't want to consider but knew she couldn't rule out. She didn't say anything to Shane about her suspicion because of the consequences if it was true, and she wanted to get proof first, which she would need special help in getting.

Shane and Emma returned to the living room and Sgt. Lincoln told Emma that she needed to go with him to the police station so she could give them a formal statement about what happened. Emma told him she just needed some time to shower and change.

Sgt. Singh nodded his head slightly toward where Lan was sitting on the couch and Emma knew he was indicating he wanted to talk to her and Shane without Lan in the room. Emma asked Lan if she could go to her room, put some clothes on, and brush her teeth and hair, and told her that she would be along in a few minutes to help.

After Lan left, Sgt. Singh said, "I have to insist that I take Lan to a safe house until we get everything sorted out."

"No way, not happening," Emma said firmly. "You want to take an eight year old girl already dealing with the death of her parents and the loss of an arm, and now an attempt on her life, and put her someplace with strangers? You can insist all you want, but the best place for Lan is still here with Shane and me."

"Emma, I'm just thinking about Lan's safety," Singh said.

"I just shot the two men who were looking for her, so I know how to keep Lan safe," Emma said. "Besides, with those two guys out of commission, I think it's a safe bet the leaders of their gang will decide to cut their losses and move on."

"I don't think you can assume that," Singh responded.

"I think Emma is right," Shane said to Singh. "You told us this gang is based in the Toronto area and Brantford is just one of the many places where it runs extraction labs. You said yourself the gang is most likely aware that it's under close scrutiny by the authorities for its immigration sponsorship scam. With what happened here last night to two of its members, it's even more police attention on them. There'll be no appetite by the gang leadership to do anything further that could jeopardize their entire operation."

Sgt. Singh didn't say anything for a moment as he thought it over and then said, "Okay, fine, Lan can stay here for the time being."

"Good. I'll get ready to go with Sgt. Lincoln," Emma said.

"I'll call Jason and have him meet you at the station," Shane said. He didn't want Emma to say anything to the police without their lawyer and friend in the room.

Sgt. Singh said he was going to leave and drive to his office in Hamilton to write some reports and as he walked to the front door, Emma followed and said, "I need you to do me a favour that will likely answer how the two men knew the code for our security system."

Emma explained to the Mountie what she wanted and went to take a shower while Shane remained in the living room with Sgt. Lincoln.

"Can you tell me what kind of trouble Emma might be in over what happened?" Shane asked.

"The use of deadly force against an intruder in your home is allowed under the law in Canada if you fear that you or someone around you is going to be killed or badly hurt," Lincoln answered. "However, while I was waiting for the forensic team to finish, I reviewed the relevant sections of the Criminal Code and things get complicated in terms of what's considered a reasonable response."

Lincoln explained the Code contains a whole list of factors to determine if an act of self-defence was reasonable, including if there were other means available to respond to the threat, whether or not you were threatened with a weapon, and even the age, size and physical capabilities of the intruder.

"Emma's description of how the one man had knocked her down and was stabbing her with a knife when she shot him would appear to be reasonable under the Code, but I'm not a legal expert and the Crown Attorney's office will have to be consulted," Lincoln said.

"At least that's encouraging," Shane said.

"However," Lincoln continued, "The fact that Emma shot the second man through the back of the knee while it appears he was trying to escape is a serious problem and she will likely face charges, especially if his lawyer starts making demands."

"That's what I was afraid of," Shane said. "I'll have to talk to our lawyer. If this guy is already facing a bunch of charges related to his gang activity, perhaps even murder for the deaths of Lan's parents, maybe there's a deal to be had."

After Emma got out of the shower, she wrapped herself in a towel, sat on the toilet seat, and held her hands out in front of her. They were both shaking and she made them into fists to see if it would stop, but when she opened them again they were still trembling. She then leaned forward and covered her face with both hands. I killed a man, she thought, I watched his brains blow out the back of his head! The Canadian Forces taught me how to kill and prepared me with the fact I might be called upon to do it, but reality is a completely different thing.

Emma was determined to put up a brave front for Lan who needed to be completely confident that Emma would do whatever it took to keep her safe. She also didn't want Shane to worry about her. However, she knew in her heart that she was going to have to spend time talking to her Psychiatrist friend, Charlene Anderson, about what happened.

While Emma wasn't worried about being justified in killing the first man, she knew that shooting the second man from behind was going to be a serious problem for her. He was trying to escape the house, so why didn't she let him go? But Emma knew the answer; she didn't want that guy out there as a continuing threat to Lan and she wanted him to pay for the hurt and fear he had caused the young girl. She didn't hesitate in pulling the trigger and blowing out his knee so he wouldn't be going anywhere but the hospital and jail.

Emma knew she had to prepare herself for the fact that she'd most likely be joining him in jail for what she did.

Chapter Twenty Two

When Shane returned to Paisley, he went to Ben's house where his friend said they would meet and Ben would share the news he had.

Before he left Brantford, Shane spent an hour in an intense discussion with Emma about how she was feeling and whether or not he should go. The police investigation into what happened at the house had been completed and Emma had yet to be charged for shooting the second intruder from behind. Shane knew the delay was the direct result of their lawyer, Jason Burke, spending a lot of time talking to the Crown Prosecutor, trying to negotiate some kind of compromise which might prevent Emma from being charged and going on trial for attempted murder.

Emma admitted to Shane that she was having some bad moments, but overall she was not experiencing any major problems dealing with what happened. Shane thought she should talk to Doctor Anderson and Emma said she was already planning to do that. Emma said she was more worried about Lan than about herself, concerned that her nightmares would return or, even worse, she would regress to the fugue state she was in during the early days of her time in the hospital shortly after her parents were killed and her arm was amputated. But Emma insisted that she and Lan would be okay and that Shane should go to Paisley.

The man that Emma killed was identified as twenty seven year old Duong Phuong and it was his younger brother, twenty four year old Quang, that she wounded.

Quang was still in hospital, under guard, following surgery on his damaged knee, and he had been charged with home invasion and attempted murder, as well as threatening, after being identified as the man who entered Lan's hospital room. It was also possible that based on Lan's statement, as well as identifying his photo, Quang would be charged for running Lan's parent's vehicle off the highway.

An arrest warrant was also issued for Duong and Quang's uncle, Hong Phuong, who was believed to be the head of a Vietnamese-Canadian crime family based in Vaughn, north of Toronto. A joint police task force with officers from the RCMP, OPP and York Regional Police raided the homes of several of the gang members, seizing opioids, weapons, cash and lab equipment for cannabis resin extraction. It was believed that Hong Phuong had fled the country.

Ben was waiting for him in his kitchen when Shane walked into the house carrying his overnight bag, which he put on the bed in the spare room. When Shane entered the kitchen, Ben got up from the table and got a beer for him and a can of Sprite for Shane.

Ben asked for an update on Emma's situation and expressed how sorry he was about what happened, something he had already done on the phone when he had called and talked to both Emma and Shane.

"The fucking authorities have to see that Emma did what she had to do to protect Lan and herself," Ben said. "She didn't know whether or not that second asshole was trying to escape. Maybe he was just going for cover or maybe other gang members were waiting outside and he was going for reinforcements."

"I'm sure Jason has thought of those possibilities in his discussions with the Crown Attorney," Shane said. "I trust him to do everything possible so Emma doesn't get charged."

Ben could see the worry on Shane's face and he thought it would be a good time to give his friend a distraction by changing the subject to the search for the person responsible for killing Shane's half-sister and her mother.

"I think I've found what the cops on the crime shows call 'A Person of Interest' that we need to check out," Ben said and then added, "It's a solid fucking lead."

Ben explained that after Shane returned to Brantford, he started asking some of the people in town that he knew about the two farm workers Biggie Gertson at the Legion told Shane about. Ben said he used the very general descriptions of the two men that Gertson had provided, hoping that would help jog a memory, but he came up empty.

"Then, by chance, I got the right fucking cashier at the grocery store when I was in there buying some supplies," Ben said.

The part-time cashier, Marie, is young and pretty, Ben said, and he figured that was why the two men lingered at her till and talked her up, and also why Marie remembered them from Ben's description and recalled some of what they told her.

"Marie told me the guy that did most of the talking said his name was Jack and that they were buying supplies because they got laid off from the farm they were working on, but were moving to new jobs near Owen Sound," Ben said.

"That's gotta be them," Shane said. "Did Marie remember anything else they said?"

"No, that's all she could recall, except she said they were funny because they sounded like the Newfies she sees on TV," Ben said and then added, "Marie's not exactly a fucking rocket scientist."

"We've got to somehow find the farm where those two guys went to work so we can ask them about the young woman Gertson overhead them talking about," Shane said.

"Way fucking ahead of you, my friend," Ben said with a self-satisfied look on his face. "I figured there can't be that many farm operations in the Owen Sound area big enough to have full-time employees. I just had to come up with a way to identify them. Then Michelle, who for your information, is both beautiful and fucking smart, came up with a great idea."

Ben said Michelle thought there had to be some kind of database of farms in Southern Ontario showing location, owner, type of operation, size and number of employees. An online search didn't come up with anything that specific, but it did list the Ontario Ministry of Agriculture, the Ontario Federation of Agriculture, the Grey-Bruce County Cattlemen's Association and the Grey-Bruce Milk Producers. Ben and Michelle split the list and called, and while the Ministry and the OFA had some of what they were looking for, they did get some helpful information from both the Cattlemen's Association and the Milk Producers.

"We told the people we talked to that we were with Stats Canada and were verifying the information provided by farm owners during the last census," Ben told Shane.

"Impersonating a federal government employee won't get you in any trouble," Shane said sarcastically.

"Fuck off, it was brilliant and got us what we wanted," Ben responded. "Both organizations gave us the contact names and locations of farms who listed themselves as having employees."

Ben said it was obvious from the number of big operations they were given that small and medium-sized family farms were disappearing, probably because they were no longer financially sustainable. He and Michelle reduced the list to only the Owen Sound area and then started calling.

"This time we said we were with a Halifax, Nova Scotia life insurance company trying to track down the long lost relatives of a wealthy man who died and left money to all eligible members of the family," Ben said.

"Very clever," Shane remarked.

"We said we were looking for a Nova Scotian named Jack, gave the description we had, and said his last known whereabouts was working on a farm in either Grey or Bruce County," Ben said.

Ben said he and Michelle spent the entire day making calls with no luck until around suppertime when Michelle connected with the General Manager of a large cattle farm near Jackson, a community east of Owen Sound. He said he had agreed to hire two easterners, Jack and Mervin, as a favour to a Paisley beef farmer who had to lay them off, but they never showed up.

"That's them!" Shane exclaimed and then asked, "Did Michelle get the name of the Paisley farmer they worked for?"

"His name is Ivan Barber of RR1 Paisley and Michelle got his phone number as well," Ben said.

"Great job, Ben!" Shane said. "If you ever decide to give up the restaurant and coding video games, you'd make a great detective."

"What and give up scooping fucking barrels of chicken fried rice?" Ben said and then added, "Michelle deserves a lot of the credit."

"Well, I owe you both dinner and a nice bottle of wine," Shane said. "But just don't pick the Chinese Buffet in Port Elgin because I hear the food all tastes the same."

"How many times have I told you that I do the Buffet insults," Ben said, trying to put indignation in his voice, but it didn't work as he and Shane smiled at each other and did a fist bump.

"So, we gonna go and check out this Ivan Barber motherfucker?" Ben asked.

"I am, but sorry Ben, you'll have to sit this one out," Shane said. "We need to be smart about this. If it turns out the farm you found is where the young woman and her daughter lived and the owner, Ivan Barber, was involved in their murders, I don't want to approach him and start asking questions when I have no authority. He could simply tell me to get lost and kick me off the property, and all I would end up doing is alerting him to the fact he's under investigation."

"So what's the plan?" Ben asked.

"I need to talk a cop into going with me," Shane said.

Chapter Twenty Three

By shortly after lunch, Shane was sitting in the small reception area of the OPP Detachment in Walkerton.

He had called ahead to make an appointment and was told that Sergeant Tyson Cornwell would be back in the Detachment shortly and had been made aware that Shane was there to see him.

While Shane was waiting, his phone pinged with an incoming text message and when he looked, he saw it was from Jason Burke. Jason, as promised, had somehow managed to get a copy of Max Ivanov's visitor log at Millhaven prison. It was a short list, only five names, four of them with Russian surnames and the other was Ivan Barber. It's the last piece of the puzzle, Shane thought. Max was the connection between my father and this Ivan Barber, the owner of the Paisley area farm where the young woman lived and gave birth

After waiting for about fifteen minutes, Shane watched out the window as Sgt. Cornwell pulled into the parking lot in a Ford SUV cruiser, got out of the vehicle with a briefcase in his hand, and walked in the front door. He was in uniform, which Shane was happy to see because it fit with his plan to have an authoritative figure with him when he went to the Barber farm.

When he saw Shane waiting for him, Cornwell said, "Hi, Shane, good to see you, come on down to my office," and then led the way deeper into the building.

Cornwell's office was small with barely enough room for a desk and two chairs, the majority of the space taken up by metal file cabinets. Cornwell set his briefcase on the top of the desk, sat down and said, "If you're looking for an update on the identity of the woman and her daughter, I'm afraid I have nothing new for you. Other than knowing that your Dad was the father of the child, so far the mother's DNA has not matched any missing persons on the national and provincial DNA Data Banks. Our canvasses have turned up nothing, but they're still ongoing."

"Actually, I'm here with something for you," Shane said.

Shane then told Cornwell about the conversation the bartender at the Legion overheard and the work his friend Ben and his girlfriend, Michelle, did to track down the two farm workers, leaving out any mention of them impersonating reps from an insurance company and Stats Canada. He explained the two workers never showed up at their new jobs, but he knew who they worked for in the Paisley area.

At this point, Shane had decided not to tell Cornwell about Ivan Barber visiting his Uncle Max in prison.

"It seems a bit thin considering it's based on what someone thought they overheard in a noisy bar," Cornwell said and then added, "But I think it would be worth checking out.

Cornwell took his notebook out of the side pocket of his uniform pants, set it on the desk and then got a pen out of his shirt pocket.

"So where is this farm located and what's the name of the owner?" he asked as he prepared to write the information in his book.

"It's not going to work that way," Shane said. "I need you to agree to take me with you when you go to see this guy before I give you his name and address."

"I can't take a civilian with me when I'm on an investigation and might come in contact with a possible suspect," Cornwell stated.

"Sure you can," Shane said. "Police officers take interested members of the public, often reporters, on ride-a-longs all the time. Just give me the waiver to sign."

"Why do you want to go with me to see this farmer, as if I couldn't guess," Cornwell asked.

"Well, to be honest, once I had the information, I had every intention of going to see this guy by myself," Shane said. "Then I realized it would be a lot better if I had someone of authority with me, like a uniformed police officer in a cruiser. I want to, if possible, shake the guy up a bit with a cop at his door asking questions. And while you're doing that, I can look at his face for signs of deception. I'm pretty good at that."

Cornwell looked at Shane for a moment then said, "Okay, you can sign the waiver and ride with me to the farm, but you stay in the cruiser while I talk to the guy."

"Unacceptable," Shane said, then stood up to leave.

"I can charge you with police interference for withholding that farmer's identity," Cornwell said.

"Well, you can try," Shane responded. "I'll just say that I came to see you with what I thought was a good tip, but then changed my mind because I decided the information wasn't really reliable."

"Okay, fine, but when we get there, I ask the questions and you remain silent," Cornwell said with frustration in his voice.

Once they were in the cruiser and on the highway out of Walkerton, Shane told Cornwell the farmer's name was Ivan Barber and gave him directions to the farm. He also told Cornwell about Barber's name being on Max Ivanov's visitor's log at Millhaven.

"My Uncle Max and Barber obviously knew each other and that's how Barber and my father connected," Shane said. "The young woman must have lived with Barber and my father met her when he visited the farm. One thing led to another and the woman got pregnant. We'll never know if my dad knew he was the father of the child, but maybe Barber eventually found out and killed the woman and her daughter."

"Let's not get ahead of ourselves," Cornwell said.

Forty five minutes later, Cornwell pulled his cruiser into the driveway of Ivan Barber's farm and parked in front of the house beside a late model GM pickup. Both men got out of the car and immediately heard a cacophony of bellowing cattle coming from two large nearby feeder barns.

"Sounds like they're in distress, maybe haven't been fed for a while," Shane said.

"For sure, something is going on with them," Cornwell said and then added, "Don't forget, I do the talking."

As Cornwell walked up the two front steps and across the small landing to knock on the front door, Shane veered off and headed for the side of the house.

"Shane, where are you going? Get back here!" Cornwell said sharply.

Shane didn't stop and said, "Just going to have a quick look."

"You can't do that!" Cornwell demanded, but Shane ignored him and walked down the side of the house to have a look at the backyard.

Once there, he saw a pile of red, round metal pipes and when he got close, realized it was a kid's swing set that had been disassembled. Shane also saw a large rusty barrel with a lawn chair sitting beside it and when he approached, saw that the barrel was being used to burn things in. It was almost half full of ashes and some materials that hadn't completely burned. Shane picked up a long stick from the ground, where he also noticed an empty bottle of vodka, and stirred around the contents of the barrel, hooking on a piece of clothing material. When he lifted it with the stick to have a look, he realized it was a piece of children's clothing.

For sure, this is the place where the woman and her daughter lived, Shane told himself, and an attempt was made to get rid of any sign they were here. He let the piece of clothing drop back into the barrel, tossed the stick back on the ground, and walked back toward the front of the house.

As Shane approached the corner of the building, he heard Sgt. Cornwell introduce himself to whoever answered the door and decided that he would wait out of sight and listen. Cornwell told the person at the door that he was investigating the murders of an unidentified young woman and her daughter, and asked if he could come in and ask a few questions.

Shane heard a gravelly male voice tell Cornwell to wait a moment and then the sound of the front door closing. About ten seconds went by and Shane figured that Cornwell was going to have to knock on the door again, but then he heard it opening.

The next thing Shane heard was the distinct sound of a shotgun being fired.

Chapter Twenty Four

Emma and Sergeant. Gurdeep Singh of the RCMP were sitting at the kitchen table in Emma's house and watching in amazement as Lan worked on a sketch on her large paper tablet.

Lan was using a set of charcoal pencils that Emma had gotten for her and she was nearing completion of a highly detailed portrait of a middle-aged Vietnamese woman.

"This is my mother, Hai Pham," Lan said as she worked on some shadowing.

There were occasional tears that ran down Lan's face as she sketched, which she quickly wiped away with the left sleeve of her pullover top. Drawing her mother had been Lan's idea and Emma was quick to encourage it, thinking it would be a good way to help Lan deal with the grief over the death of her parents.

"I'm doing my father next," Lan told Sgt. Singh. "Doing the drawings will help me remember what my parents looked like. And then I'm doing Emma, then Shane, and then you, if I can remember what you look like when you're gone."

"I would be honoured," Singh said. "Your sketches are incredible. You are a very talented young girl."

to regret for a long time because I put Lan's life in jeopardy. Before he left for an out of town trip, Shane reminded me to remove the sticky note on the fridge door which had the code written on it that came with the system and then I was to go to the control panel and change the code to something personal I would remember. I didn't do it right away like I was supposed to. That sticky note was still on the fridge last time you were here Maggie."

"What are you suggesting? That I memorized the code and gave it to those two men?" Maggie said with a surprised look on her face.

"I'm not suggesting it, Maggie, I'm telling you that I know you did it. Emma said in a matter of fact tone.

"That's ridiculous!" Maggie exclaimed. "Why the hell would I do that!?"

"I suspect for the oldest reason in the world," Emma responded. "Money."

"I can't believe you're accusing me of this! You're crazy!" Maggie said and even through the heavy makeup she normally wore, Emma saw that the woman's face was beet red.

"What happened has seriously affected you, Emma," Maggie continued. "You're paranoid. I'm not going to stay here and be accused of something I didn't do. I'm leaving!"

Maggie grabbed her coat off the back of the chair and was going to walk out when Sgt. Singh, who had remained silent until now, said, "You're not leaving, Maggie, sit down."

"You can't keep me here!" Maggie protested.

"I can and I will," Singh told her. "Please sit down, I don't want to have to handcuff you."

"Before you waste your breath protesting some more, let me tell you something," Emma said to Maggie. "I asked and Sgt. Singh agreed to get a warrant to search your bank accounts. He found three accounts that you set up in your name at banks other than the one you normally use, and where you made a cash deposit in each one of nine thousand five hundred dollars, which is just below the ten thousand limit when the bank has to report it to the authorities. Where did you get that much cash?"

Maggie didn't answer, she just stared at Emma, the normally pleasant look on her face had changed to one of fear, and Emma noticed that Maggie's hands were trembling.

"You don't want to say?" Emma asked and then continued, "Okay, I'll answer for you. The two members of the Vietnamese gang who were trying to find Lan somehow found out that you were handling her file. They approached you and offered, what? thirty thousand for the address where Lan was living?"

Maggie still didn't speak, but tears were trickling down her face in two dark streams because of her heavy mascara.

Sgt. Singh then said, "Maggie, the only way to help yourself is to confess voluntarily and tell us everything you know."

After another moment of hesitation, in a soft and shaky voice, Maggie said, "My husband has been out of work for almost a year and we've been falling deeper and deeper into debt trying to live on my pay. We're about to lose our house and will have to declare bankruptcy. I was heartbroken that I would have to do that and make my kids live in some shitty apartment. I don't know how they knew that, but they offered forty thousand dollars for the address where Lan was living."

"Who approached you?" Singh asked.

"I was sitting in a coffee shop when a man in a suit sat down and asked me if I was interested in a way to get some immediate help with my financial problems," Maggie replied. "I don't know how he knew that information and he wouldn't tell me."

"Did he give you his name or a business card, anything that would identify him?" Singh asked.

"No, he just said he represented a Vietnamese-Canadian businessman, but this guy was not Vietnamese," Maggie answered. "He was a middle-aged white guy."

"Okay, Maggie, you're going to have to go with me and make a formal statement," Singh said and then stood up.

As they started toward the door, Maggie turned to Emma and said, "I'm so sorry, Emma. I was desperate, and I only agreed because the man assured me they just wanted to warn Lan again about cooperating with the authorities. I told him that you and Lan had grown close and he said that if they also threatened you then you would make sure Lan remained silent."

"Come on, Maggie, you knew that was bullshit," Emma said with a look of disgust on her face. "You knew they were likely coming here to kill Lan and me. For someone whose job was to protect vulnerable children, you had no problem throwing that all away. I'm going to do whatever I can to make sure you go to prison for a long time."

With tears running down her face, Maggie started to say something else, but Emma held up her hand to signal to Maggie not to bother and with that, Singh put his hand firmly on Maggie's arm and led her out the front door.

After they left, Emma sat down and felt like crying herself. She had really liked Maggie and her apparent devotion to her job, and felt sad that she was willing to throw all of that away. Emma knew that she had been lucky and that, unlike Maggie, never had to worry about money. The Canadian Forces didn't pay very well, so at the time she lost her leg and left the army, she was barely scrapping by, but her parents were always there to help her out. She lived at home and when her parents died, they left her the house mortgage-free and a sizable life insurance payout. As a nurse, she made a good salary and Shane always covered half the household expenses. On one hand, Emma could sort of understand Maggie's desperation over losing her house and being able to financially care for her kids, but Emma could never betray a trust for money.

Emma opened the door and went into Lan's room where the young girl was sitting cross-legged on her bed working on the sketch pad on her lap. Emma sat on the bed beside Lan and asked, "Any chance I can get a hug?"

Lan set her charcoal pencil down, turned, and after the two embraced, asked, "I heard angry voices, Emma, is Maggie okay?"

"Maggie has to go away, so we won't be seeing her again," Emma answered.

"Why?" Lan asked.

Even with her limited experience with kids, Emma knew they asked 'why' a lot because of their insatiable curiosity and you had to be cautious, but specific, in answering if you wanted to avoid a series of followup 'whys'.

"Maggie got herself in trouble with the law and has to leave her job, but it's nothing for you to worry about," Emma answered and then readied herself for the next question.

"Oh, okay," was all that Lan said and returned to her sketch pad.

Emma was a bit surprised there were no further questions but thought that perhaps Lan was too preoccupied with her own problems to wonder about anyone else's. If that was the case, it said a lot about what was going on in the young girl's mind.

Chapter Twenty Five

The sound of the shotgun being fired out the front door of the Barber farmhouse sent a shock wave through Shane's body and he instinctively stiffened and pressed his body harder against the side of the building.

Shane then heard the front door slam shut again and he decided to dare a quick peak around the corner. He saw Sergeant Cornwell lying on his back on the ground in front of the steps up to the front door. The front of his shirt was tattered, exposing the bulletproof vest underneath, the upper half riddled with small entry holes from the shotgun pellets.

The vest had saved the police officer's life, but Shane could see blood running down the side of Cornwell's neck, which meant that because the shotgun shell hit near the top of the vest, some of the pellets must have penetrated Cornwell's neck and perhaps his throat. If that was the case, Cornwell was in very serious trouble and would need immediate medical attention.

Shane didn't know when or if Barber was going to come back out the front door, so he had to act quickly. He left the protection of the side of the house, hustled over to where Cornwell was on the ground, and knelt to check on the officer's condition. Cornwell was semi-conscious, his eyelids closed but fluttering, and he was moaning softly. Shane saw that four or five shotgun pellets had punctured the right side of Cornwell's neck in a cluster from the bottom of his jaw to the top of his collarbone, but miraculously, none had entered his trachea sending blood into his lungs and impacted his breathing.

"Hang on Sergeant, I'm going to get you some help," Shane said and then leaving his cane on the ground, he got up, grabbed the top of Cornwell's vest at his shoulders and dragged him backwards behind the rear of the cruiser for protection.

Shane pulled his phone from the back pocket of his jeans and had just dialed 911 when he heard the front door of the house start to open. Shane left the call open and put the phone back in his pocket, hoping that Bruce County had the advanced 911 system which could track his location without him on the phone to tell them the address.

After the phone was back in his pocket, Shane reached across Cornwell, removed the officer's Glock service pistol from its holster, and looked over the trunk of the cruiser, through the rear window and windshield, at the front of the house. Barber was on the front step, a large leather travel bag in his left hand. As soon as he saw that the police officer was no longer where he left him, Barber started to reach behind his back with his right hand.

Shane figured Barber was likely going for a pistol that was stuffed in the back of his pants, so he quickly stood up, pulled the slide on the Glock to put a bullet into firing position and then walked down the side of the cruiser.

With the pistol held out in front of him in a two-handed grip, Shane called out, "Barber! Drop the bag and put your hands in front of you where I can see them!"

Barber froze in place, surprised to see a stranger pointing a gun at him. Shane took a step forward and exclaimed, "Do it!"

Barber dropped the travel bag from his left hand, moved his right hand from behind his back, and then held both hands in front of him, palms up.

"Who the hell are you!?" Barber said loudly.

"I'm the guy who's going to take you into custody for the murder of a young woman and her daughter, and for the attempted murder of a police officer," Shane stated.

"I don't know what you're talking about!" Barber exclaimed. "I didn't kill anyone and was only protecting myself when I was accosted by a police officer."

Shane ignored Barber's claim of innocence and said, "I'm also the brother of the young girl you callously strangled and buried."

Barber decided that denial wasn't going to get him anywhere so he said, "That's impossible, that young girl was my daughter. What's your name?"

"Shane Daniels. My father was Ed Daniels." Shane stated, keeping his gun pointed at Barber even though his arms were starting to get tired.

"Ed Daniels!? I knew that whore was lying to me when she said the kid was mine!" Barber said angrily. "She and your father were fucking behind my back. I welcomed the bastard into my home and he betrayed me."

"How did you know my father?" Shane asked, even though he was sure he already knew the answer.

"He was the brother of an old friend of mine," Barber said and then decided to put his hands down at his sides. Shane noticed the gesture but decided to let it go, for now.

"You were a friend of my Uncle, Max Ivanov," Shane said and the confirmation staggered him a bit as he thought about how he just couldn't escape the twists and turns of his father's life.

"You obviously met Max in Russia. Were you a criminal like him?" Shane asked.

"A criminal? No, I was an officer with Military Intelligence," Barber replied with some indignation in his voice.

"If that was the case, why are you here, on a beef farm near a small town in Ontario?" Shane asked.

"I may have overstayed my welcome in Russia and Max said this was a good place to live out of the way, so here I am," Barber answered.

"And, of course, Ivan Barber isn't your real name," Shane stated.

"It's close enough," Barber said flatly.

Shane noted that Barber kept taking quick glances at the gun in Shane's hands, probably thinking that if he kept Shane talking, the weapon would become dead weight at the end of his arms and he would have to lower it, at least momentarily. It would give Barber an opening to attack. Shane knew he should get Barber secured using Cornwell's handcuffs, but he had a couple more questions he wanted to ask while Barber was still talking.

"What were the woman's and my sister's names?" Shane asked.

"She went by Elizabeth Rowlands and the daughter was Rebecca. She said her real name was Iliana, but that could have been false as well," Barber replied. "She was a whore who was smuggled into Canada from Moscow and given to me as a gift by Max, who somehow arranged it from prison."

Shane was again staggered by the information, realizing that both his father and Uncle Max were directly tied to a double murder.

"Why did you kill them if you thought you were the child's father?" Shane asked and he could feel his anger starting to build and his self-control over his temper slipping away.

"They were starting to be a problem," Barber said. "She wanted to spend time away from the farm and she wanted the kid to have friends and to go to school. I blame your father because he was always whispering ideas in her ear. And just as important, she was getting too old for my taste."

The nonchalant way Barber talked about murdering a young woman and a child made Shane's face burn with anger and hate, and he knew he had to get the Russian in handcuffs and into the back of the cruiser before he did something stupid, like pulling the trigger on his gun.

Shane then saw that while Barber was answering the last question, knowing what he said would shock the man holding the gun on him, he had moved his right hand behind his back.

Shane stiffened, tightened his grip on his gun, and said, "I know you have a gun in the belt at the small of your back. Trust me when I tell you that I know how to use this gun and if you go for your weapon, I won't hesitate to shoot you, so remove it from your belt by just the grip and put it on the ground."

Barber made no move to comply and continued to have his right arm behind his back.

"You need to understand that I have no choice but to get away from this place," Barber stated. "I'm a dead man if I'm forced to stay because Russian agents will find a way to get to me in prison. And if I'm sent back to Moscow, I will disappear for good as soon as I walk off the plane. I have nothing to lose."

"Yes you do, your life, because I will shoot you," Shane said as he took another small step toward where Barber was standing.

Barber suddenly brought his right arm from behind his back and raised the pistol in his hand toward Shane.

But before he could aim, Shane fired his gun twice in rapid succession, a double tap as it's known, and both bullets hit Barber in the chest. The Russian staggered back from the impact of the bullets, dropped the gun in his hand, and went down to the floor of porch.

In the distance, Shane heard the sirens of approaching emergency vehicles.

Epilogue

The fact that Emma and I had both killed a man within the span of two weeks resulted in a lot of sharing of emotions as we worked together to deal with what happened.

I was a mental wreck almost immediately after I pulled the trigger twice and killed Ivan Barber at the front door of his farmhouse, even though I knew I had to do it or he would not have hesitated to shoot me. It didn't matter if it was justified as self-defence; as soon as I did it, I started asking myself if I shot Barber because I wanted to kill him for murdering the half-sister I would never get to know. Is it possible that subconsciously Barber became a stand-in for my father, who I tried to kill for his involvement in the murder of my mother, but couldn't do it?

When I was done with the explanations, interrogations and signing of statements that followed what happened at the Barber farm, and Emma and I finally had some time alone, I became distraught when I told Emma about my thoughts.

Emma became upset, almost to the point of anger and said, "No! No! Never, Shane! You would never intentionally set out to kill someone. You're not wired that way and never have been!"

I responded emotionally to what Emma said by stating, "I keep asking myself, if I didn't have some kind of intention of shooting Barber, why didn't I take the gun I knew he had in the belt at the small of his back, put him in handcuffs right away, and then ask my questions? Why did I keep him standing on the porch? Why did I allow him to lower his hands? I knew I was facing a man who was likely very desperate, but I let him stand there and talk. Was I hoping he would go for his gun so I could shoot him?"

"Shane, everything that happened was in the heat of the moment," Emma said. "You know as well as I do because of what happened to me, that there was no time to analyze what we were doing. You were desperate for answers about your murdered sister and the man who killed them was standing right in front of you. You didn't think to yourself, 'I need to put this guy in handcuffs so he doesn't try anything', you just started asking questions. That's it, end of story. Please stop beating yourself up."

Emma was probably right, but I was still having a tough time dealing with it. I did take some solace from the fact that if I subconsciously intended to shoot Barber right from the start, I would have also known in the back of my mind that if I killed him, then the answers to some questions would die with him.

And that turned out to be the case. Russian officials were cooperative up to a point, but all they would say officially was that Ivan Barber's real name was Ivanovitch Barbarov and he was wanted for theft of state funds. They didn't confirm that he was an officer with the GRU.

The Russians also claimed they were unable to find any information on a missing Moscow teenager with the first name Iliana and said that if she was a prostitute, well, prostitutes disappeared all the time.

After checking from Owen Sound all the way south to Kitchener-Waterloo, Police could find no record that Iliana, under the name Elizabeth Rowlands, gave birth in a hospital. But they expected that, considering Ivan had basically kept her captive on his farm.

They eventually tracked down the midwife in Owen Sound who helped Iliana with a home birth and she admitted that she was paid on the side for her silence about anything that might have been said to her by the young girl she knew as Elizabeth. But the midwife said it didn't matter anyway because Elizabeth remained mostly silent about herself during their appointments, other than to say that Mr. Barber was her uncle and he agreed to take her in while she had the baby, and that she got pregnant by a boyfriend who was now out of the picture.

So, sadly, any family of a young woman who said her name was Iliana will never know what happened to her and I'll always be bothered by that. Russia didn't want to repatriate the bodies, so after receiving permission from the proper authorities, I had Iliana and Rebecca buried in my family's plot at the cemetery south of Paisley.

Police managed to track down information on the two men who worked for Barber on his farm. A search of Barber's home office turned up employment records for Mervin Gatlin and Jack Warren, who listed their previous address as Hantsport, Nova Scotia. The

Mounties in Nova Scotia were contacted and they found an uncle of Mervin's in Hantsport who said that although Mervin had been gone for several years working on farms across Ontario, he always called at least once a month because he was the only relative he had. The uncle said he had not heard from Mervin in some time and he was starting to get worried. No relatives of Jack Mercer were found.

Police talked to the Owen Sound area farmer that Ben and Michelle had found and he confirmed that he had agreed to hire Jack and Mervin based on Ivan Barber's recommendation, but they never showed up.

Police believe it's more than possible that the two missing men are dead, likely killed by Barber because of what they knew about Iliana when they were working on the farm. An extensive search of Barber's property turned up nothing, so the whereabouts of the two farmhands remains a mystery.

While I was dealing with the mental conflict I felt over shooting Ivan Barber, both Emma and I were under a lot of stress waiting to find out if Emma would be charged for shooting the second intruder who had broken into our house to get at her and Lan.

It had already been determined that it was clearly an act of self-defence under the law when Emma used a legally registered firearm to shoot the man who was trying to stab her. The problem revolved around Emma shooting the second man from behind.

It appeared the police, after consulting with the Crown Attorney, were prepared to charge Emma with aggravated assault and let the court determine if she was guilty or not. If she was found guilty, Emma could spend up to fourteen years in prison.

But our brilliant lawyer and friend, Jason Burke, made sure that didn't happen and we will be forever grateful for his help. Jason successfully convinced the Crown Prosecutor handling the case that it didn't matter where in the house the second intruder was located when Emma shot him, he had already tried to assault her, was armed, and remained a direct threat to her and Lan. Jason told the Prosecutor they had little chance of convincing a jury otherwise and a trial would be a waste of time and money. Thankfully, the Prosecutor agreed and actually told Jason he was personally glad he could make that decision given what Emma had gone through.

In the midst of dealing with the shootings, Emma and I never lost sight of the most important thing going on in our lives and that was our relationship with Lan.

We met on several occasions with Maggie Sawyer's replacement from Family and Children's Services, a much older woman, June Cummings, who said that the Vietnamese-Canadian couple in Brantford was still willing to take Lan, even though they were aware of what happened at our house. There was no reason to believe Lan was in any further danger considering that one suspect was dead, another was under arrest in hospital, and police had carried out a series of raids and arrests which effectively shut down the gang interested in finding Lan.

The problem was that Emma and I wanted Lan to continue living with us and even though we both wanted what was best for her, I knew that Emma loved the little girl and would be heartbroken when she left. As for Lan, she became very upset when June explained to her what was happening and that she would be back later in the day to pick Lan up for the move.

Lan looked up at Emma with tears in her eyes and said, "I want to stay with you Emma, why can't I do that?"

Emma knelt, hugged Lan, and said, "Both Shane and I would love you to stay sweetheart, but they feel that it's important that you be with people from your own culture and background."

"I don't care about culture!" Lan protested and then lifted her right arm stump and asked, "How is culture going to help me live with this?"

After Emma got up from hugging her, Lan turned to June and said, "Don't I get a say on where I live, because I want to stay with Emma and Shane. Please, please, don't make me go!"

"Can't we come to some sort of arrangement?" I asked. "Emma is the most qualified person to help Lan adjust once she has her prosthetic. Lan has already been registered to attend a nearby school, which has the advanced learning classes she requires, and we would be more than happy to take Lan to any Vietnamese cultural events held either here in the city or nearby."

"Okay, okay, I know when I'm beaten," June said with a big smile on her face. "This is obviously where Lan wants to be and I'm going to make that happen."

"Yay!" Lan exclaimed and hugged both Emma and me.

The look of joy on Emma's face had me again amazed at how a little girl had transformed a tough, no-nonsense, former army bomb disposal expert, who said she didn't want kids, into the woman standing beside me. I think adoption papers were in my future.

Lost in all that had happened recently was the decision I had to make about undergoing surgery to get an artificial knee. Because of my situation, the surgery was risky and there was a good chance the artificial replacement wouldn't work and my leg would have to be amputated.

I wasn't sure what I wanted to do and even though my cane has been part of who I am for a long time, I would be more than happy to toss it away.

I had to decide, but it wouldn't be today.